Straw & Gold

A REALM OF REVELRY FAERIETALE

CHELSEY ANN TOMPKINS

Written by

CHELSEY ANN TOMPKINS

A Realm of Revelry Series
Curse & Spindle
Straw & Gold

A Conduit of Light Trilogy
A Conduit of Light
A Baron of Bonds
A Blightress of Wrath

For all the Rumple fans. Enjoy, dearie.

*Also for Des—I spun it into a faerietale
and look how perfectly it fit.*

Author's Note

This book for adults contains the following: murder, death of a lover, chronic anxiety, blood, attempted sexual assault (mild, not graphic), and sexually explicit acts between consenting adults

Pronunciation Guide

Characters

Morella, MORE-EL-UH
Killian, KILL-EE-AN
Fedir, FED-EAR
Céad, SEE-AD

Language

Céaduah, SEE-AD-DO-UH
Moh Dhóches, MOW DOUGH-SHEZ

*Author's note: the language of the Changelingfae is based off Scottish Gaelic. I have much respect for this language and without a human translator, I decided to have Céaduah *inspired* by Scottish Gaelic instead of attempting a direct translation.

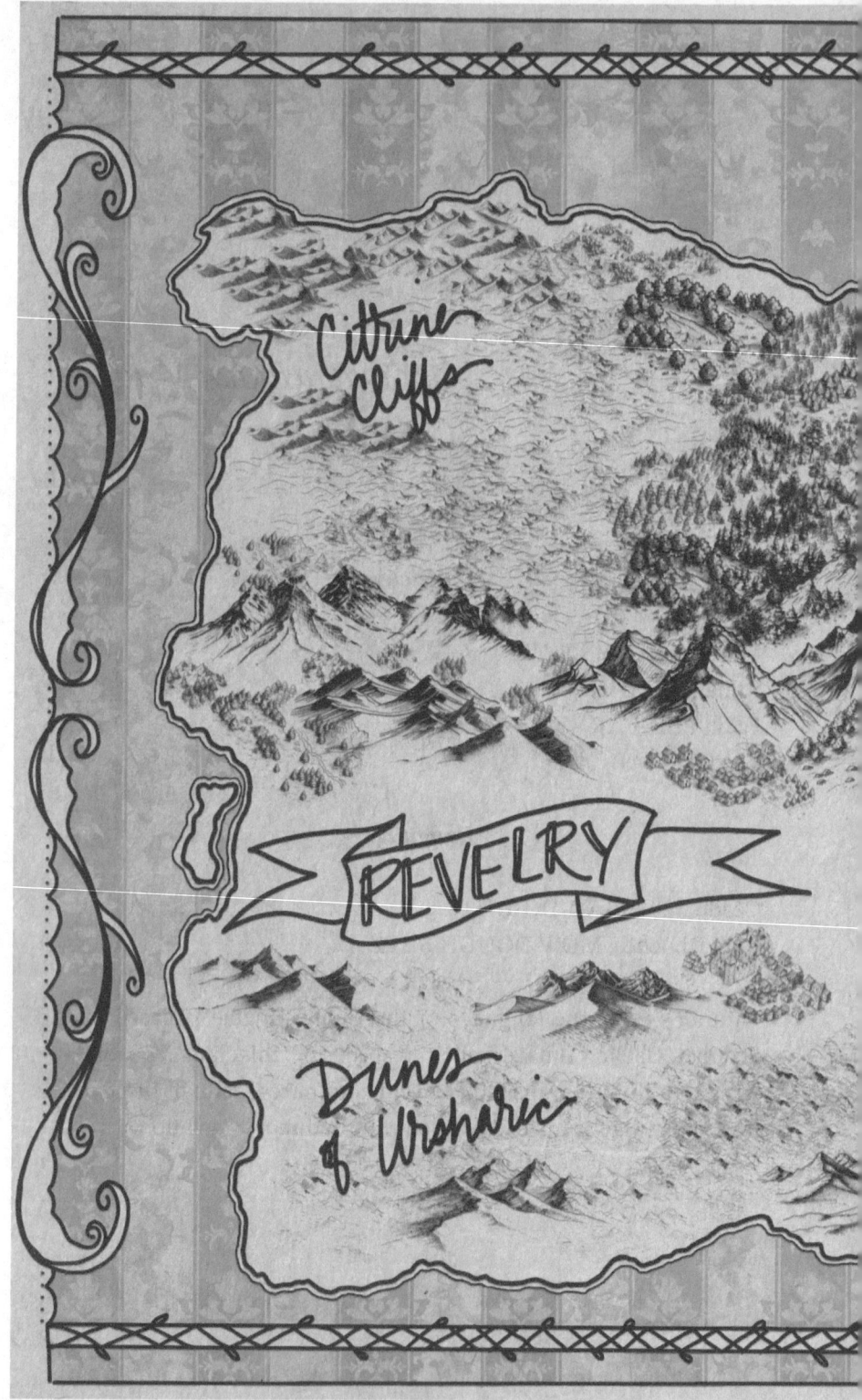

Silver Isle

Moonstone Wood

Brakish Wood

Heartstone Wood

Havenshire

Riche

Songbird Cove

CAT

Morella

MY BROTHER TUMBLED FROM THE SKY IN THE EARLIEST light of dawn. He shifted from a raven, black as night, to a Ravenfae Prince—exhausted and keeled over in the morning dew. His hands dug into the grass as his breath came in labored, heaving gulps.

His wife, Seraphine, tossed their daughter into my arms and bolted from the door without a word.

"Papa!" my niece squealed, reaching out her chubby little arms.

"Yes, Avici, just give your papa a minute with your mama," I grunted, doing my best to keep the soft downy feathers at her back from slapping me in the face. Her name meant *fledgling* and she lived up to it in her many attempts to fly at only two years old.

I plucked the very last honeysuckle blossom from the vine growing over the cottage door, distracting her enough to keep her on my hip while I watched my brother recover.

Korven, Ravenfae Prince of the Brackish Wood and Curse-bringer of Revelry had just returned from a night of a Cursed Moon. On these nights, the Cursebringer brought curses from the Veil to all those unlucky to receive them and all babies born under that moon. A Cursed Moon occurred twice a year, but sporadically. This moon came only four weeks after the first, and the hardship of the Cursebringer of Revelry remained plain on my brother's face.

For eighteen years, my much older brother had taken on the duties of Cursebringer from our mother, the Ravenfae Goddess. The duty would have gone to me as her original heir, but by the time I had turned ten, Korven had decided he would take over the Cursebringer burden instead.

I looked on in guilt and shame as my brother and his wife reunited on the soft path that led to their cottage door. Seraphine pulled him into her arms, kissing his forehead many times before trailing down his cheek—all the way down to the bramble berry tattoo inked along his neck.

He let himself fall to her lap, still breathing hard from his long night. I stepped out of the stone doorway and unfurled my black feathered wings tipped in gold. Avici dropped the yellow bloom in her little hands and reached for the sky. "Let's fly, little bird," I laughed.

Holding her back to my chest, I launched into the lightening blue, understanding perfectly well that my brother and Seraphine were going to need a minute. Or by the looks of the kiss she just gave him...several.

My niece giggled in unbridled joy as I flew over the trees in the midst of exchanging their summer green to the rich colors of autumn. In precisely two minutes, we would arrive at our favorite cliffside in Moonstone Wood—the one where the golden rays of sunrise glinted off a waterfall, lighting up the valley below. Three minutes of flight was my current limit, so a rest watching the sunrise was the perfect start to the morning.

I landed softly, nestling Avici into my lap as we sat near the cliff's edge. She pointed to the stream of water gushing over the side of the rocks, ensuring I was watching for the spark of golden light to appear. Her cry of joy was bright as the sun when it glinted off the spray of water, and I laughed with her, soaking in my last few hours before I'd leave her for months.

Within twenty-four hours, I'd begin my journey, traveling across the acres of Moonstone Wood to enter the realm of the Changelingfae, right to the Citrine Cliffs of Revelry. The trek would take three whole days, but only because my brother and I would travel by carriage instead of flying—something I'd never have the strength to do.

In three days, I'd be married.

In three days, I'd be bound to a husband I'd never met.

In three days, I'd be queen.

I wasn't sure which I was excited for most.

CHAPTER 2

Killian

IN THREE DAYS, I'D BE MARRIED.

If she showed up.

If she didn't finally get the cold feet I'd been relying on to excuse us both from the contract I'd penned thirteen years ago.

The Ravenfae Princess had written to me thirty times since then, and I'd gotten rid of every letter, sealed and all with the wax stamp of the Brackish Wood.

At what point would she rebel?

At what point would she realize that marrying a complete stranger was...stupid?

I'd gotten what I needed from that betrothal contract and left an escape clause so she could grow up from a mere fifteen years old and easily break it.

Why didn't she break it?

"You look a bit vexed."

I turned my attention away from the day's accounting reports and closed the book. Folding my hands across my chest and leaning back in my leather chair, I sighed.

Fedir continued polishing his blades, laying each one flat on the small table by the fire as he ran his cloth across the sharp metal.

"Marriage is already not agreeing with you," he continued, shifting his gaze to find me frowning his way.

"She is a foolish, fanciful princess, Fedir. It's the only explanation for why she is still coming." I flicked my own blade from my baldric and began to polish away invisible specks.

He chuckled. "She's already gotten under your skin." He replaced his blades, adding, "I'm going to enjoy this."

"You're going to do what you can in the next three days to get me out of this," I replied sharply, throwing my dagger across the room. It embedded into the leg of the table with a loud *twang*.

"Missed, Your Majesty," he goaded.

"You sure?" I replied, sitting back once more, resting my hands behind my head. "Check the right leg of your breeches, Captain."

He pulled my knife from the table and inspected his leg, finding the slice across the leather and poking his finger through. "Are you sure you need me to waste my time looking for a way out of this contract? Your precision is better than mine."

"I've been over it so many times," I admitted, rubbing my face. "*She* is the only one who can break it."

He chuckled, rising and stretching, flinging my knife right back to my desk, impaled in the corner. "Maybe she'll get one look at you and run."

"If only I were so lucky," I grunted, scratching at my overgrown beard.

"Or," he continued, "maybe she'll get one look at those luscious red locks and fall to her knees like the rest of them." He winked and moved to the door.

I glared at his back, stringing my fingers through my long, flaming red waves. I could use a shave. And a haircut.

"Three days left as an unmarried man, Killian," he called, heading out the door of my study. "If I were you, I'd find some company before I was tied down for the rest of my life."

"If you were me, Fedir, this castle would have its own brothel."

I heard his chuckle in the hall as the door swung closed.

In three days, I'd be bound to a wife I'd never met.

In three days, she'd be queen.

I wasn't sure which I was dreading most.

CHAPTER 3

Morella

"THIS ONE IS FOR SCRAPES AND SMALL WOUNDS," Seraphine said, handing me a jar of blue paste. "And here's one for blemishes."

My trunk was already full, but my sister-in-law was wrapping her jars of salves in brown paper, tucking them tidily into each corner. She made the ointments using crystals she found in Moonstone Wood and sold them at the Forestfae market once a week. I admired how everything Seraphine put her mind to, she accomplished. There was very little I could attempt with her level of success.

"And this one..." she trailed, taking a small jar of something clear but viscous from the top shelf of her cabinet, "is for you and your husband-to-be."

"What is it?" I asked, taking it from her and shaking the contents.

"Well...when you and your husband are...intimate, this will enhance the experience for the both of you."

"Ah." I blushed, wrapping the jar tightly and shoving it into the top pouch inside the trunk. Lowering my voice, I asked, "And where exactly do we put it?"

Her gaze shot across the room to my brother who was

holding my niece upside down by her ankles as she laughed and hiccuped. "Just...wherever you feel comfortable with the king touching you." She twisted her lips, closing the trunk lid. "Maybe introduce it a few weeks into your marriage, after you've both had some time to adjust to each other."

I pulled her into a tight hug. I'd never had a woman in my life to speak to about men, and love, and romance, until my brother had brought his soon-to-be wife home to our castle in the Brackish Wood. I loved her the minute I saw her, and we'd been thick as thieves ever since.

But the woman I thought of as my sister was not fae like us. Seraphine was human. She would live a *human* lifespan.

But not if I could help it.

I pulled back from her arms, taking a deep breath. "I'm going to miss you so, so much."

She smoothed her thumbs over my cheeks, holding onto my face. "I'll miss you too, my sweet girl." She sniffed, then her mouth pursed into a serious line. "Don't let your husband give you shit, and don't lose sight of who you are and were born to be. You will be queen, and with that comes a responsibility to your people. Bring them your many talents and they will love you."

I nodded. "I'll try."

"No, you will succeed," she commanded. "I believe you can do anything, Morella, Ravenfae Princess of the Brackish Wood."

I fell into her arms again, overwhelmed with her endless love and the hope she continued to give me over the last thirteen years of my life.

First, I'd get my husband to help me transform Seraphine into faekind.

Then, *together*, he and I would bring more prosperity to our kingdom and live happily ever after.

I ASKED MY BROTHER MANY QUESTIONS ON THE CARRIAGE ride through Moonstone Wood. As always, Korven accommodated my curiosity about the curses woven for the people of Revelry—the same curses I would never have to deliver. He spoke of various ones with some sounding dreadful, others more irritating than anything.

"And the crew won't suspect the captain's curse?" I asked. "Wouldn't it be obvious?"

"I doubt it," he answered, watching the grassy fields out the window. "Do you really think pirates would notice if their captain's heart was missing from his chest?"

"But how will he live? That's a pretty important part of his body."

Korven laughed, shrugging. "How did Seraphine live in a spirit form until her curse was broken?"

I sighed and watched the Citrine Cliffs draw closer. "I'll miss her so much." I turned to him, smiling. "I'll miss all of you."

My brother tensed, whispering, "We can turn around, Morella."

"What?"

"We can still get out of this contract. You know the escape clause. We can turn this carriage around and send word to the king."

I frowned, about to speak, but Korven stopped me, taking my hands. "You signed that marriage contract when you were fifteen years old. There's no shame, or guilt, or anything fucking wrong with making a different choice at twenty-eight. All you have to do is write to him. Explain you've changed your mind and you will be a free woman."

"I don't want to be a free woman."

"You made the choice when you were a child! You've never even met the man!"

"And how long had you known Seraphine before you slipped a ring on her finger, hmm?"

He shook his head. "That's—that's different."

"Why? Because you knew her when you were ten?" He remained silent and I continued. "Look, brother, I hear you. But I want this. I can do good things as queen and I am *sure* I can love my husband."

"What if he's covered in boils?"

"Then I'll write to Seraphine for a salve."

He laughed, pulling me to his seat and tucking me in under his arm.

I rested my head on his shoulder and pulled a handful of thistle nuts from my pocket, munching on each one and savoring the saltiness. "Do you think I can be a good queen?" I asked.

He kissed the top of my head, taking one of the nuts I offered him. "I think you'll be the best queen. And we will miss you, too. Dearly."

WE ARRIVED AT THE TOWN OF CENMAR JUST AS THE SUN kissed the horizon. Korven secured our room at an inn called *The Miller's Daughter*, planning to stay the night before he would fly home in the morning.

The marriage contract between the King of the Citrine Cliffs and the Ravenfae Princess of the Brackish Wood had been odd in numerous ways. For one, there was a direct escape clause. The contract said that upon or after my twentieth year, if I were to spin a cop of yellow wool into yarn and send it to the king, I could choose to release myself from the contract.

Another oddity was that no family was to accompany me to my wedding. I would be allowed to visit, of course, and they could visit me, but the first three months of the marriage was to be without the comforts of visitors.

Lastly, after that first three months, either the king or I could withdraw from our marriage entirely should we choose to do so. We could go our separate ways of our own will, even if the other did not agree, and no longer be married.

Not only was that rare among marriages in Revelry, it was probably one of the only real reasons Korven hadn't shipped me off to the Silver Isle to be hidden from my betrothed. That last bit gave him hope that I'd return home when I discovered the disappointments of married life to a stranger.

In our room, Korven pulled the wine-red velvet dress from my trunk, holding it up to get another look. "I guess it's time," he mumbled with a frown, draping the soft gown over the dressing screen.

I stepped behind the panels, shaking with excitement as I slipped out of my dressing gown and into my wedding dress.

The gown had draped sleeves that hung off my arms and the back was cut low with a few ties. The front bodice boasted no embellishments except for the cut, which was a heart-like shape that pronounced my breasts without becoming too vulgar. It had been custom made to accommodate my wings and even though Seraphine had steered me far away from choosing the traditional white gown, she had been surprised at my choice of dark red velvet.

I stepped out from the screen and twirled around. "Well? What do you think?"

"Beautiful," he hummed.

I beamed and turned so he could help with the ties. "I truly wish you could be there. When the first three months are over, you and Seraphine and Avici can travel to my castle and we will have a proper celebration!"

He tied the strings and turned me around. "And if we arrive and find you miserable?"

"I won't be!"

"How will I know?" He squeezed my shoulders. "You said you'd write once a week, but what if this king is a right asshole and reads them beforehand or forces you to say nice things?"

I laughed loudly, grabbing onto his arms. Korven had always been protective—overly so—but I knew it came from a place of the love he had for his only sister. The same one he had practically raised in place of our cursed mother.

"Korven," I started, lowering my voice sternly, "do you really think I'd let my husband do such a thing? Fuck that."

"Add something to each letter then. Find a way each week to just...tell me you're alright."

I frowned at the idea. I was leaving for many reasons—one of them was getting out of the reach of the long arm of my brooding brother. I loved Korven with all of my heart, but I needed to be able to fly on my own.

I sighed. "Thistle nut."

"What?"

"Thistle nut." I shrugged. "Each letter, I'll find a way to add *thistle nut* and you'll know I'm not being coerced to write nice things."

He nodded, pulling me in for another tight squeeze. "Alright. Thistle nut it is. Promise?" He held out his pinky and I wrapped it with mine.

"Promise."

CHAPTER 4

Killian

I STOOD IN THE ROOM MY SOON-TO-BE WIFE WOULD occupy for her stay in my kingdom. Fedir leaned against the doorframe, flicking his hunting knife between his fingers. The last few maids fluffed the pillows on the enormous four-poster bed and stocked the dressing table with a brush, hand mirror, and hair pins.

"The sun sets," Fedir taunted.

I glanced out the west-facing windows, a pit forming in my stomach. I turned over my shoulder. "What are the chances she doesn't show?"

Fedir tossed his knife in the air, catching the handle and placing it back in his boot. "Zero, Your Majesty." He folded his arms and grinned mercilessly. "Word is, a carriage traveling from Moonstone Wood has arrived at The Miller's Daughter in Cenmar. And two Ravenfae were in it."

I scowled, grunting in acknowledgement. The maids took that as their cue to exit, swiftly shuffling out the door, each leaving a smile for my rake of a Captain. Fedir stepped further into the room, nodding in silent approval at the comforts I'd made for Morella. "It's only three months, Killian," he murmured, tracing his hand over the golden brush at the dressing table.

"Three months is all I have left, so you'll excuse me if I don't want to spend them with a stranger."

"Will you bargain with her?" he questioned softly.

"I don't know."

"You might as well."

"What if there's something wrong with her?" I shook my head in exasperation. "What princess would agree to this?"

He shrugged. "In her letters, she seemed sane."

I turned on him. "You read them?"

"One or two over the years."

"I told you to burn them."

"I did burn them...eventually."

"You're a bastard."

He laughed, grabbing my shoulder. "And you were a fool to get rid of them so easily. There might have been all kinds of scandalous secrets in those letters."

He moved to leave, but I stood in his way. "What did the letters say?"

"Oh," he drawled, "this and that. She likes to spin."

"Spin?"

He nodded, picking at his teeth. "On a spinning wheel. She claims to be very good at it."

I huffed. I'd heard as much from her mother when drafting the contract. "What else?"

"I really don't remember. This was years ago."

"If she's not insane, what else is wrong with her?"

Pausing a moment, he gasped, snapping his fingers. "What if she's ugly?"

I gave him a skeptical look.

"Like really, *really* ugly. Absolutely hideous. Think about it... a Ravenfae Princess is basically a bird, correct?"

"Raven," I amended.

"Right, and she probably has a beaked nose and beady black eyes. In fact," he continued, standing tall and laughing, "I'll bet you fifty marks she has the feet of a crow!"

"*Raven*," I rebuked.

"Whatever. Point is, you and I have never actually seen a Ravenfae. Fuck, this entire kingdom and over half of Revelry hasn't—your contract negotiations with the Ravenfae Goddess was done by letters, even. So, what if she's half a bird and then here comes along a contract of marriage to a far-distant king?" He tsked and shook his head. "Sounds like the best offer she's going to get."

I nodded slowly. "Maybe you're right."

"Two hundred marks says you'll find her unattractive."

"I don't want your coin if you're wrong."

"I'm sure I'm not. I do want your coin, though, if I'm right."

"Fine," I said in exasperation. "Just go await the carriage and bring her to the throne room when she's ready so we can get this ceremony over with and get to the drinking."

He bowed out of the room replying, "Tick tock, my king."

My heart softened a little as he left and my mood lightened.

Yes, if she was hard to look at, this would be much easier. I would let her down gently and after a few months of marriage, I'd convince her that we were just not compatible. Maybe then I could set her up in a nice country house nearby and she could be taken care of for the rest of her life, regardless of what happened to me.

I took a deep breath and pulled on the lapels of my gold embroidered jacket. Morella's room was ready and beautiful. I wanted to make her life comfortable in the castle while she was in it, and hoped the hapless girl would find some peace in the beauty of the castle and its lush grounds.

I swept my hand through my red waves, borrowing a pin

from her table to tuck them away for the ceremony. I was ready to meet my betrothed and start the process of letting her down easy.

CHAPTER 5

Morella

KORVEN KISSED MY CHEEK ONE LAST TIME AND reminded me of my promise before I shifted and flew off to the castle gate. I soared up to the few clouds in the sky, my golden feathers glinting in the last sliver of sun. In my Ravenfae form, my feathers were tipped in shimmering gold—a contrast to Korven's pure raven black and our Ravenfae Goddess mother's—which were tipped in silver.

But when I shifted, I became a golden raven entirely, which had always seemed odd since for my mother it was not so. She and Korven looked almost identical as ravens, and I stuck out like a glinting piece of jewelry in any sky.

My future husband was a Forestfae, contrary to the Changelingfae he ruled over in the Citrine Cliffs. I wondered what the story was there.

Actually, I was obsessed with someday discovering what the story was. I'd spoken to Fiola about it before. She was the Forestfae Goddess who ruled over Moonstone Wood and raised Seraphine. All I'd gotten from the exchange was a a hefty *harumph* and mumble about his unusually great power to change one thing into another.

Whatever mysteries I had yet to discover about my royal

husband, I was dying to know them. I was dying to know *everything* about him.

What did he look like?

What were his hobbies?

Did he care for his subjects?

Did he have a favorite nut?

Was he a good kisser?

These questions and many more had been wandering through my mind on occasion for the last thirteen years. I was naturally very curious about my betrothed and even more so ready to get him to like me. *Hopefully* fall in love with me so that I could convince him to change Seraphine, and then we could really begin our lives together.

As the castle gates neared, I descended, shifting back to Ravenfae and startling the three guards on duty.

"Hello!" I greeted them cheerfully. "I am Princess Morella, Ravenfae of the Brackish Wood!"

All I received were blinks and gaped mouths.

Finally, one of them bowed, clearing his throat and replying, "Of course, Your Highness! I'm sorry, we were startled by the... the..."

"Shift," another replied, unlocking the gate and allowing my entrance.

I chewed my upper lip before internally scolding myself for doing so and possibly smearing the dark red lip stain. "My apologies for startling you, uh, good sirs. Please direct me toward the castle doors so that I may attend my own wedding."

The last one chuckled, followed by an elbow to the ribs.

"It is us who apologize, Your Highness. You see, we expected you to arrive in a carriage and expected you to be wearing..."

"White?" I suggested.

"Well, yes. And again, I apologize, but we've never seen a Ravenfae and you-your wings..."

"Are gold?" I provided.

"Yes, yes, so sorry."

I tilted my head, studying them further. Each guard was draped in a deep blue with golden swirls embroidered on their jackets. Swords draped at their hips and each sported long hair tied back at the top of their heads. The most surprising thing was that each of them had one eye of blue and one of gold.

"Are you..." I started, stepping back to take a better look. "Are you brothers?"

The youngest seeming one piped up again. "Yes! Good eye, my queen!"

He was jostled again in the ribs.

The oldest spoke up. "Please allow me to introduce myself and my brothers." He pointed to himself and bowed. "I am Tairyn, second to Captain Fedir." He gestured to the next one. "This is Zarif, and this is Cordyn. We have been tasked by his Royal Highness King Killian of the Citrine Cliffs to escort you and your belongings into the castle so that you may settle before the ceremony begins in one hour."

I nodded slowly, taking in their names and doing what I could to commit them to memory. "My trunk is on its way to the castle. I didn't want to wait for it to get here before I arrived."

The man I knew was Tairyn led the way toward the castle doors while his brothers continued guarding the gates, bowing ridiculously low as I left.

I surveyed the structure as he led me through a well kept courtyard. The last blooms of summer struggled to stay on their vines and the wide trees hinted at autumn with their orange tipped leaves. The castle was long and rectangular, each end sporting a tall circular tower with a pointed pinnacle. The stone was gray, but each tower top glimmered in a coppery shimmer.

"These are beautiful grounds," I commented.

Tairyn nodded, adding, "His majesty takes great pride in employing many of his subjects at the castle. There are twenty gardeners who I will pass along your compliments to, princess."

"Please do!" I squealed. This was happening. *This was really happening.*

"Oh!" he exclaimed as we came to enormous, wide-open copper doors. "His Majesty has sent Captain Fedir to guide you to your rooms. I will leave you, princess."

I gave my thanks and stepped into the castle, my hands clasped in front of me with a wide grin and wide eyes as I surveyed the elegant foyer. Brilliant flourishes of gold overlaid the woodwork of the doors and stairs. Gold was even inlaid into the wooden floor. I spun around in awe, admiring my new home.

"Princess Morella?" A man stepped casually from beside the door.

I gasped, clutching my chest. "Yes?"

He stepped forward. "You're Princess Morella?" He glanced over my wings and red gown, stopping at my honey gold eyes. "Morella, Ravenfae Princess of the Brackish Wood?"

Confused at his insistent questioning, I answered yes again.

A hefty, stuttering laugh escaped his chest. Followed by another. And another until his hands pressed to his knees and he wheezed in fits.

Awkwardly, I peeked out the doors, sure that Tairyn had been mistaken.

"I'm so sorry, Your Highness," he wheezed, struggling to recover.

"I don't understand," I stated, irritation rearing its head. "Have I done something funny?"

"No, no." He waved a hand, rising to his full height. "You've done nothing." He wiped his eyes. "I just owe someone a very large sum of marks."

"Oh," I murmured, taking him in as he regained his composure.

Not quite as tall as my brother, he was built similarly so with strong arms and a lithe body. His dark skin paired handsomely with his low-cut curls, but the most surprising of his features was that his fingers ended in golden skin. Not a tanned gold like Seraphine when she'd been out collecting Moonstone in the summer, but actual shimmering gold.

He caught me staring, and held them out in front of his body for me to get a better look. "Have you ever seen a Changlingfae, Your Highness?"

I shook my head.

"Well, it just so happens, I've never seen a Ravenfae. So please,"—he bowed deeply, sweeping his hand out in front of his chest— "allow me to properly introduce myself. I am Fedir, Captain of the Guard to his Majesty, King Killian of the Citrine Cliffs." He rose, taking my hand and planting a light kiss on my knuckles. "It is a pleasure and my honor to meet you, Princess Morella. I look forward to serving as your Captain as well."

I took my hand from his and inclined my head. "A pleasure." I turned, once again admiring the beauty of the castle. "May I ask you something, Captain?"

He bowed once more. "Of course, Your Highness."

I took a deep breath. "Will the king react as you did when he sees me?"

His brows shot up and his smile grew. "Uh, no." He cleared his throat. "No, there's no possibility of that, princess."

"If I am offensive in my presentation of myself, please—"

"Princess Morella, he will gut me three times through if he ever hears word of my initial, rather rude reaction to meeting you for the first time, so it is I who ask you to save my life and never speak of it to him." He cleared his throat again, offering his hand to shake. "It is my own idiocy that has made you doubt your appearance. You are a stunning woman, and I, as you will soon discover, am a blundering fool."

I took his hand, nodding. "I believe you."

He chuckled. "Please allow me to escort you to your rooms where you can freshen up before the ceremony."

I agreed and he turned to the long stone staircase lined in a rich burgundy carpet. My nerves were finally getting to me as I silently followed. He pointed out the many paintings and corridors, mentioning something about each tower, and referring to the long hall we walked as the Royal Wing.

I half listened, second guessing my choice of gown. But Seraphine had promised my future husband could find no fault in the drape or color. Surely the captain had not laughed at my wings...those they would be expecting. And by the amount of gold in the castle, I doubted the shimmer of my feathers had put him off.

I straightened my spine and took a deep breath. *Don't lose focus, Morella.*

"And these are your quarters, Your Highness," Fedir said, interrupting my attempts to regain my confidence.

I half-listened and stepped inside a beautiful room draped in pale blues and, as was the castle theme, golden accents. Our marriage bed was large and well-stocked with soft blankets and pillows. I peeked into the bathing chamber to find a copper tub and more modern accommodations.

"This is a lovely room," I said, feeling refreshed.

"His Majesty will be relieved to hear you say so. He ensured it would have all the comforts a queen could want."

"He is very kind to do so," I remarked.

"I will leave you to freshen up, Your Highness, and come to retrieve you for the ceremony at a quarter past. When your trunk arrives, it will be brought here."

"Thank you, Captain."

"Please, call me Fedir, if you'd like."

I nodded and closed the door behind him as he left.

Alone in our room, I wondered at the lack of personal items from the king. I saw no evidence he lived here at all and I certainly looked. I even peeked under the bed for shoes, or forgotten books, or old swords—anything that would hint at my husband's hobbies or personality.

Figuring this was a room he had furnished as a new start for us both, I sat at the dressing table and tucked the flyaway hairs back into my braided bun. I dabbed at my lips, smoothing out the dark red stain and inhaled deeply.

"This is it, Morella," I told my reflection. "Wife, Queen, Lover, and Seraphine's Only Hope." My stomach churned and I took another deep breath, shaking my head. "It will all turn out," I encouraged. "You've wanted this for so, so long." I gulped and smiled at myself. "Take it. It's yours."

Soon, a soft knock came to the door and when I opened it, Fedir was back, this time dressed in a formal jacket. Two servants brought my trunk into the room and Fedir offered his arm for me to take.

On the arm of the Captain of the Royal Guard, I headed downstairs to the throne room to marry the man I'd been betrothed to for almost half of my life.

CHAPTER 6

Killian

SHE WORE RED TO HER OWN WEDDING.

She wore *red*.

And her wings were tipped in gold.

CHAPTER 7

Morella

THE KING OF THE CITRINE CLIFFS WAS FUCKING *gorgeous*.

My mouth parted and I let out a sigh of relief and excitement as he stalked down the aisle of the throne room. Hundreds of people had gathered, crowded together to form two sides of the room—most straining their necks to get a good look at their future queen.

The man didn't *end.*

He took up the entire walkway with broad shoulders, a height that towered well above my own, and a wide chest somehow wrangled into a cream shirt and dark blue jacket.

When he reached us at the throne room doors, Fedir spoke up. "My king, may I present to you Morella, Ravenfae Princess of the Brackish Wood, Daughter of Reshina, Goddess of the Veil, and sister of Korven, Cursebringer of Revelry."

The king frowned at the captain who smirked in return until his face lit into a smile that swept across his dimpled cheeks. Killian turned his attention to me, his eyes trailing over my body as I did the same to him.

Finally coming to my senses, I bowed, dropping my hand

from Fedir's arm. "It is a pleasure to finally meet you, Your Majesty."

I rose and clasped my hands in front of me, waiting for his next move.

He rubbed a hand over his mouth, once again having a silent conversation with his captain, who struggled to contain his laughter. And once again, I felt out of the loop.

Fedir regained his composure, cleared his throat and stepped back.

Offering his arm, the king finally spoke in a deep voice that rang through the hall. "Shall we?"

That was it? That was all he could say?

I frowned, but took his arm anyway, embarrassed at how long the three of us had stood there.

A chill of cold sweat slipped down my back as the guests made room for both of us to walk down the aisle as complete strangers off to marry each other.

"Stay fucking focused, Morella," I whispered under my breath.

My soon-to-be husband glanced down at me, his red locks sneaking loose from the golden pin holding them back. "What did you say?" he grumbled as we reached the dais and the priest from the Temple of the Goddess of the Veil.

"Tell you later," I whispered back, my eyes locked on the priest who began his anointing of our marriage to be blessed by the thirteen fae Goddesses of Revelry.

Half-listening, I bit the inside of my lip repeatedly, keeping my head straight and side-eying the man next to me as much as possible. Annoyingly, he avoided looking in my direction at all, which was also quite convenient because I could study him much better if he kept to his profile.

His skin was a soft porcelain hue with a few freckles lining his nose and across his cheeks. His eyes were the brightest shade of blue, like a Moonstone itself. He was certainly very hairy.

Ravenfae didn't grow much facial hair, so seeing such a bushel of a beard was fascinating. I wanted to run my fingers through. Would I catch something? A crust of bread? A small twig? A long-lost trinket?

He squeezed my hand rather hard as it was tucked into his arm, and I jerked my face away from where I'd been blatantly staring.

"Sorry?" I asked.

The priest cleared his throat, repeating, "Do you share this man's hand in marriage along with his bed, meals, and faith in the wisdom of the Goddesses of the Veil?"

"Yes, I do," I exhaled quickly, reddening from my lack of attention.

The man turned to Killian. "And do you share this woman's hand in marriage along with her bed, meals, and faith in the wisdom of the Goddesses of the Veil?"

He nodded.

"Seriously?" I scoffed in a whisper.

He turned his head and scowled down at me.

More lip chewing began but I held his gaze.

Once again, the priest cleared his throat, muttering, "Your Majesty, it must be—"

"*Yes,*" he gritted, staring me down the whole half second of the word.

So this was it, then. I'd married *this* man.

He took a ring from his pocket, slipping it onto my finger. At least he had good taste. An emerald-cut citrine stone sat poised above a golden band with delicate feather details gracing the side, ending in two mossy green, circular stones.

I barely had time to wiggle his own band of gold onto his finger before the priest announced, "Ladies and gentlemen, Changelingfae of the Citrine Cliffs, may I present to you King Killian Brehan and his wife, Queen Morella Brehan."

Polite clapping followed and what I was sure was a cheer from my new Captain of the Guard.

"Kiss your bride, my king!" the priest called, and if looks could kill, he would have been stone dead by the way my new husband scowled.

The king took a deep breath and I looked on, utterly confused. He bent and quickly pecked my lips in the most chaste kiss I'd ever received.

It was worse than Brekkan Dioltry's, who'd only known where to stick his parts and nothing else that summer we'd turned nineteen.

"Seriously?" I questioned again.

My husband ignored me, turning us both and walking us back down the aisle, still holding my hand in his arm, still barely acknowledging my existence.

CHAPTER 8

Killian

"It's a good thing she's beautiful," my captain chuckled, winking in my direction.

I downed the rest of my wine, slamming the golden goblet on the table and nodding to the closest servant to refill it.

As she left, I took another gulp. "Is it, Fedir? Is it a good thing? You said she'd have the feet of a *bird*."

"*Raven*," he corrected, leaning back in his chair, balancing on two of its legs with his hands behind his head. We watched the new queen twirl around the crowded room, passing from person to person as the dance allowed, laughing and stumbling slightly all the while.

"Did you really get a good look at her feet yet?" He winked again and I kicked his seat, sending him tumbling back behind the long table set up on the dais in the throne room. His booming laughter followed as he regained himself and I silently studied the queen.

Her laughter rose above everything else in the room, including the song of the finest musicians the Citrine Cliffs had to offer. Her subjects laughed with her, cheering and drinking— over half the room already too far into their wine for the amount of time left in the celebration of our marriage.

I called one of the servants over, whispering in her ear, "Have blankets brought up from storage. Pillows if we have them. Prepare for a crowded hall tonight and a larger breakfast than usual in the morning. We're going to have a lot of hungover and hungry guests."

She bowed and scampered away. Fedir stood and downed the rest of his wine. "For the sake of the Goddess, will you go and dance with your wife, Killian?"

"You know I won't."

He bowed in mockery. "Then allow me." He swept his hand out in front of him and I gave a curt nod.

I heard her laugh again in that delightful, joyous sound as Fedir joined her, arm in arm, skipping around in a circle. He led the dance, helping her with the steps she didn't know. When the music faded, she curtsied, revealing that she most definitely did not have scaly bird feet.

As another dance began and Fedir handed her off to someone else so he could chase down the latest of his bedmates, I rose and began to circle the room. Many congratulations and drunken toasts followed. I shook hands, patted backs, and caught more than one unruly stumble as I found my way to a darkened corner of the hall, out of sight, but in a position to carefully watch her.

Three songs later and well into the darkest hours of the night, she wiped her brow, laughing with her partner and shaking his hand. Charmed, he kissed it and bowed low, almost falling to the wood floor before she caught him, delighted, and the picturesque bride on the night of her wedding. Helping him to a bench seat, she poured herself a goblet of water, swallowing the contents in a few long gulps.

With one more wipe of her hand across her forehead, she undid the ties at her hair, sweeping the black locks up at the back of her head and pinning them away from her neck and face. Another potential dance partner offered his hand as the next song began, but she turned him away with a shake of her head and hand over her heart. Taking one last gulp of water, she lifted her red skirts, toeing across the room swiftly.

To my horror, she headed directly toward me, never once looking my way. Arriving in the dark alcove, she turned and leaned back against the cool stone, not two feet from me, her wings tucked in at her back.

She huffed a loud exhale, wiping at her neck. "Will all our celebrations be this exuberant?" she asked, turning to face me in the dark.

"How did you know I was here?" I asked, stepping into the light.

She grinned beautifully, her golden-flecked eyes playful. "I've known your placement the entire night. Is it not my duty to know where my husband is?"

"It is not," I replied, my foul mood at war with the way her cheeks flushed in the dim flicker of candlelight in our corner.

Shaking off my rudeness, she offered her hand. "Will you not dance with me, husband?"

"I do not dance," I replied.

"Even on your wedding night? With your bride? You do not dance even then?"

"What bride wears red to her own wedding?" I asked before I could stop myself.

She frowned, looking down at her skirts and pulling the dark fabric out on display. In a pout she said, "I love this color. And I look good in red."

"Didn't say you didn't." *Shit.*

Another flush crept up her cheeks.

Three months.

I had three months left of this and she had hundreds of years.

What was the harm in one dance?

No. I shook my head.

She wouldn't know the harm in one dance. She wouldn't know the invisible dagger in one slip of my hand across her waist, one brush of breath across her temple.

Plan A was for her to back herself out of the contract.

Plan B was to ensure she wouldn't miss me when I was gone.

CHAPTER 9
Morella

I DROPPED THE FABRIC OF MY SKIRTS IN THE SILENCE that followed. So far, that was the nicest thing he'd said to me.

I cleared my throat, my heart hammering with a new tactic to hear more kind words from my husband's lips. "I'll admit, I'm exhausted after three days of travel." I laughed lightly. "Would it be rude for us to retire a bit early?"

Looking relieved, he offered his arm. "I will escort you upstairs, then."

Giddy at the prospect of getting him alone in our room, I quickly folded myself into his side, unable to deny how well we fit together.

Loud whistles and cheers followed us as we walked through the crowd. I didn't miss the wink from Captain Fedir, nor the scowl on my husband's face. He did smile occasionally on our stroll through our guests. I caught each of his small grins, wondering what I could do to get him to smile like that at me.

The halls of the castle were well lit by the copper sconces along the stone walls. Servants and more than a few couples from our wedding darted in and out of rooms and dark corners of the castle.

He didn't say a word, only led us toward the staircase that fed us to the long corridor where our room awaited. Excitement pumped through my veins.

This was my first night as a married woman.

Goddess, it had been what felt like centuries since I'd been touched by a man. Not that I expected him to touch me. More than likely, I'd guess he'd rather wait until we were more comfortable around each other.

But if he did want to touch me, I wouldn't have a single hesitation.

My wings shifted of their own accord at the thought, the left one smacking him in the back of the head.

"Sorry," I rushed, lifting my hand to pat his hair. "My wings have a mind of their own sometimes."

He stopped in front of our door, rubbing his head. "It's fine." He opened the door with a copper key before pressing it into my hand and gestured for me to enter.

"Thank you." I lifted my skirts and stepped inside, recognizing my large wooden trunk, still packed as I had requested.

"If there's anything you need, pull this cord and a servant will be with you shortly," he instructed. "I wish you a goodnight, Morella."

He pulled on the door to shut it and I jammed my foot in the base. "Are you not tired?"

He cocked his head, nodding. "Not as exhausted as you, I'm sure, but yes, I will retire as well."

Confused, I opened and shut my mouth. He moved to pull the door closed again, but again, I was in the way. "Do you have duties to attend to first?"

His confusion matched mine as he replied, "No...I will go straight to bed."

I gestured behind me. "This is your bed."

He peered around the door, speaking slowly. "That's your bed."

"And yours," I amended, matching his tone.

"Morella, this is your room." Turning, he pointed to the door across the hall. "Mine is here."

"Yours is..." I stared dumbfounded, squinting at the door carved with flourishes and forest trees.

Killian coughed into his hand. "Well, goodnight."

I removed my foot from the door, nodding in a daze. "Goodnight."

The latch locked in a resounding click that seemed to echo through my head, and I was left alone on the night of my wedding.

I WASN'T SURE HOW LONG I STOOD OUTSIDE HER DOOR.

Long enough to pick up the light rustle of her red gown as it fell off her body and onto the floor.

Long enough to hear her enter the bathing chamber.

Long enough to hear her rummage through her trunk, likely finding...whatever she wore to sleep.

Long enough to see the light go out under her door.

Long enough to convince myself to turn around and wait to see her tomorrow.

THE DRAGGING SOUND BEGAN AT AROUND TWO IN THE morning from what I could tell. I rose suddenly from the damp sheets where I'd been having another bout of nightmares—one after the other after the other—as was routine.

I wiped my face, quickly tying my hair back and glancing at the clock. Surely the guests had gone by now or were fast asleep in their makeshift beds on the floor of the great hall.

The long scrape of something heavy began again, and I bolted from my bed, headed for Morella's room. I threw my door open and stepped into the hall, still dimly lit by one candle every other sconce.

The Queen of the Citrine Cliffs hunched in a crimson night-dress, lace cuffing the floor-length hem and thin silk pronouncing her curves. Her back was to my door as she pulled again at her trunk, dragging it across the floor. Her wings shifted and flared every foot she gained.

"What in the name of the Goddess are you doing?" I all but yelled, grabbing her arm to turn her.

She let go of her trunk and the look on her face would have drowned any other man. "I'm bringing *my* things to *our* room. What does it look like?"

"*Our* room?"

"*Our* room."

I glanced behind me, still bleary, half wondering if I was dreaming this. "You're trying to sleep here?"

She turned back to her trunk, continuing to drag it across the floor. "I live here," she said with a grunt, adding, "With you." She backed into me as I blocked the door. "We're married, lest you've forgotten in the six hours it's been." Adopting a saccharine grin, she cooed, "Be a dear and open the door a little wider, husband."

"*Morella*," I gritted through clenched teeth, "I don't want you to live here."

Her frown pursed into a pale thin line. "I gave my vow that I was sharing your bed and that makes it my bed as well." She pointed into the room. "Just look at the thing! We'll each stay on one side and practically have our own estates."

Her wings were stronger than I expected, unfurling into my face and forcing me back. Quickly, she pulled her trunk the rest of the way inside before taking a look around.

"This will do nicely. I assume we have a bathing chamber?"

She waved a hand flippantly in my direction. "Never mind, I'll figure it out."

She padded across the room, taking in every piece of me that was evident. Reaching the bed, she leapt across the sheets, tucking herself into one side.

Still in a stupor, I stood in shock, glancing from her trunk to her in my bed as if I couldn't quite understand how they'd gotten there.

"Morella?" I whispered harshly, shutting the door behind me.

She didn't answer in the consuming dark.

And in my stupidity, I didn't insist she answer back.

CHAPTER 11

Morella

THE SOUND OF BIRDS CHIRPING INCESSANTLY WOKE ME, and as much as I struggled to tune them out, the singing came with my name beside the bed.

"Morella."

I blinked blearily, rubbing my eyes.

No, I was not mistaken.

My mountainous husband peered down at me from the side of the bed. His face was close—too close to not have a purpose, and I grinned, unable to stop the warm excitement that burst through my veins.

I was *married*. To *this* man.

I stretched my arms over my head and let out a groan. "Good morning," I cooed, ensuring I was not at all covered by sheets in my thin nightgown. "Did you sleep—"

"Why didn't you break the contract?" His voice was dark and deep, matching the frustration on his face.

"What?"

"Our marriage contract, Morella. Why didn't you break it?"

"I..." Sitting up, I pulled the covers a little closer.

In the early light, it was easier to make out the details of our room. Dark midnight blue accents in the curtains and tapestries left a feel of old secrets and rich history.

"Morella," he commanded, grabbing my chin and turning my head to face him again.

"I didn't want to break it," I answered truthfully.

"Why? You were fifteen. Fifteen-year-olds don't just willingly give away their futures to men they've never met."

I frowned, wiggling out of his hold. "Didn't you read my letters?"

"I burned your letters."

"But why?" I whined. "I wrote them for you to get to know me."

"What could I possibly have learned from a fifteen-year-old— seven years younger than me?"

"But I sent more as I got older!" I yelled, now hotly offended. This was too damn hard. It didn't need to be so hard. We were married. Done. Finished. What was there to worry about now?

He folded his arms and leaned back in the chair by the bed. "And what are you now? Nineteen?"

"I'm twenty-eight, jackass!"

"Ah, the language of maturity," he jeered.

I snapped my mouth shut. Fine. He wanted to begin our first day this way, and I wasn't going to fight him and give him the satisfaction he obviously enjoyed from our first spat.

I hurled the bedding in his direction, pulling myself out of the sheets and scooting to the far side of the massive bed where I hopped out, throwing open the curtains before storming off to find the bathing chamber.

Rounding the foot of the bed, I stopped short.

Our room was enormous, easily as big as Seraphine and Korven's entire cottage. The bed I'd slept in remained in the middle of the room at the far wall. But next to it was a dressing screen wrapped around another, smaller bed that I knew hadn't been there the night before.

"What's that?" I asked, pointing at the new arrangement.

Killian rose from his chair, picking it up and placing it back at his desk near the door. "That's your bed."

I pointed again to the bed I'd slept in last night. "This is my bed."

He shook his head. "You may insist on sharing a room, but we are not sharing a bed."

My face fell. "Why not? We don't have to...you know."

He leaned against his desk, shoving his hands in his pockets. "No, enlighten me."

"You *know*," I lifted my hands in the air and gestured to the bed wildly. "What two people tend to do when they share a bed together."

His face remained stone as he asked, "Which is?"

In an exasperated groan, I flipped open the lid of my trunk, searching for one of the new gowns I'd commissioned for my days as queen. Yanking it out, I slammed the lid closed with my foot, wincing at the sound of breaking glass. "Don't pretend you don't know what fucking is, Killian. You've got the word written all over you."

He watched me open the lid again to search inside for which jar had broken. "Do I now?" he murmured softly, coming nearer.

I began pulling dresses, undergarments, and jars out by the handful, searching for the one that was bound to be leaking over everything, despite Seraphine's careful packing.

"What are these?" he asked, bent next to me. I jumped, snatching the tiny jar of gel Seraphine had given for intimate moments with my husband. I glanced over the contents and scoffed. "Don't worry about that one," I replied sweetly. "We *won't* be using it."

"We?" he replied.

I ignored him, searching in each corner until I found which jar was broken.

Two jars, actually.

"Goddess fucking dammit!" I cursed, carefully pulling out the broken bottom of a salve for small cuts along with the broken jar of thistle nuts I'd stashed away until I could bring more.

The nuts were covered in blue goop and utterly inedible. All I had left of them were in the pockets of my traveling dress from yesterday.

Killian emptied a basket filled with extra blankets and brought it over to my continued cursing as I pulled more glass from the trunk.

"Here. Put the pieces in this and be careful with them."

I sighed, but did as he said, adding, "Oh, you care suddenly?"

"I don't want blood and...whatever this is all over my room."

"Our room," I corrected under my breath.

I continued to carefully lift each piece of broken glass, knowing most of these gowns would need to be laundered before I could wear them.

He rose and cleared his throat. "Your bed is here. Your wardrobe is there." He pointed at a new wooden cabinet I swear hadn't been there the night before either.

"Did I sleep through servants bringing these in?" I opened the doors, finding it empty.

"No," he said, folding his arms again.

"But then how did they—"

"You'll find the bathing chamber behind this door." He pointed at the blue door beside the second bed. "And you'll find this door leads to my study." He gestured to the door painted in gold next to the enormous fireplace that took up most of the wall.

"*Our* stu—"

"No, Morella, I will not be sharing my study with you. Your vows did not promise that."

I folded my own arms at my chest. "*Our* vows," I added, just to smile at his irritation.

He strode to the door leading to the hall. "I expect you to be ready in fifteen minutes. Someone will come to retrieve you for *our* breakfast."

I grinned happily at my success at him using the word.

He poked his head back in as he left. "Don't get so excited. 'Ours' meaning the entire castle staff and guests will be there, too."

He chuckled and shut the door on my scowl.

Twenty minutes later, I was already five minutes late.

The servant he had sent up to retrieve me waited politely at the door to our room as I scrambled in and out of the bathing chamber, tossing my things every which way out of my trunk, looking for proper shoes to coordinate with my midnight blue dress.

I slid across the wood floor, calling, "Just one more minute, please!"

She curtsied and said softly, "Your Majesty, perhaps you could use some assistance?"

"Oh, no," I laughed, "I really am almost—" I found my second shoe, cursing at the blue salve gooped at the heel. Falling to the floor in a slump, I rubbed my face, exhausted from long days of travel, a night of dancing, and a vexing husband.

I had lain in that room for two hours the night before—tossing and turning, growing angrier by the minute before I'd decided to take what I wanted.

And I wanted to share my bedroom with my husband.

Judging by the rising flush to my cheeks as I pictured his face, I wanted to share much more, even through his incredible talent of making this harder than it needed to be. But I never did back down from a challenge. And Killian was a challenge I had no choice but to win.

"Would you prefer to wear these, Your Majesty?" the woman said, holding out a pair of yellow slippers, gilded in pearls.

"Perfect!" I shouted, sliding my feet into them and rising from the floor. "Right. Thank you, er—"

"Alista, my queen." She curtsied again, clasping her hands in front of her.

I thanked her another time, giving her a good once-over. Ringlets of gold framed her head in striking contrast to her mahogany skin. With wide eyes and full lips, I recognized her as the servant who had captured Fedir's attention on the dance floor.

"May I?" she asked, gesturing to my frizzy braid.

Nodding, I sat at Killian's desk, making note that I'd need to drag the dressing table into our room as well.

Alista hummed a sweet song as she braided my thick black locks, taming them into something far more queenly than I'd ever be able to achieve. When she finished, she added, "Just one moment, Your Majesty."

She rushed out of the room and across the hall. I peeked through the door to find her rummaging in the wardrobe of the room I would have been occupying if Killian had his way. Pulling out a crown of simple gold and citrine, she placed it on my head. "There," she sighed, "you're ready for your first day as queen."

I stole a glance in the mirror, admiring her work. "Alista, would you be able to help me more often? I mean, at least until I get the routine of things around here."

"Queen Morella, I have already been assigned as your personal maid."

"By whom?"

"King Killian, of course."

"Of course," I echoed.

As I followed Alista through the halls, I tried to memorize each path that led to the lavish dining room, overfilled with people. Some of our wedding guests mingled with plates full of cheesy eggs and some kind of black meat.

Each bowed as we passed and I nodded, attempting my first impression to be the right one. I'd been born a princess, but that didn't mean the customs of the Brackish Wood were that of the Citrine Cliffs.

The Ravenfae, though respecting the royal children of the Ravenfae Goddess Reshina, were not exactly formal in their treatment of those in high ranks.

I followed Alista's bouncing golden curls to my seat near the head of the long dining table—right across from my scowling husband.

"You're ten minutes late," he scolded, pushing his empty plate forward.

Captain Fedir remained silent beside him, but watched us both with interest.

A plate filled with eggs, fruit, and rounded slices of the black meat was set down in front of me. Lifting my fork to poke at the runny beans and what looked like steamed tomatoes, I replied, "My clothes were more covered than I'd thought. That ointment got onto everything."

I took a bite of what seemed to be a harmless piece of toasted bread and met Killian's gaze with a polite grin. He watched me chew, his brilliant blue eyes darting from my mouth, to my crown, down to my dress of midnight blue where my breasts were hinted at in the square neckline.

Calling Alista to his side, he murmured something in her ear to which she nodded, bowed, and left. Fedir's eyes followed.

Killian wiped his mouth and rose from his seat. I bolted from my own.

"I must begin the day's dealings," he said, pushing in his

chair. "Fedir will begin your tour of the castle and grounds if you'd like."

"I wouldn't mind waiting for you to finish so you could give the tour instead."

His eyes looked me up and down again. "Fedir will suffice. I have meetings to attend and farms to visit."

He turned to leave but I was already there at his side, taking his arm. "I'd like to visit as well!"

His eyes darted to my hand on his soft linen sleeve. Goddess, he was warm. And his forearm was *huge*.

Taking my hand gently, he squeezed my fingers, murmuring low, "Perhaps another time, Morella."

He left without another word and Fedir joined my side. "Would you like to finish your breakfast before we begin, Your Majesty?" he asked.

"No, thank you," I sighed, suddenly queasy as I watched my husband leave me once again.

CHAPTER 12

Killian

"THE HERD'S BEEN WANDERIN' AGAIN, YOUR MAJESTY. More than usual, but Beireoir here's got some good days left in 'im."

I ruffled the ears of the hound and he licked my hand in response.

Nodding in silence, I surveyed the herd of white sheep dotting the hillside. "They gave a good clip this spring. We should have more than enough wool to last through until next year." Petting Beireoir again, I switched to the Changlingfae tongue. "And the moss stores?"

The herder known simply as Cú replied with a grunt.

"Good, good," I said, switching back to the common language in Revelry.

I folded my arms, brushing my hand over my forearm where Morella had touched me three mornings ago. In that time, I had swept away right after breakfast, ensuring Fedir would give her tours and lectures about every part of the castle and grounds while I managed to visit the few dozen farms of my kingdom. Each night, I returned just before the darkest hour, finding Morella already asleep in her own bed.

And now, I had no more excuses to be away from the castle. Away from *her*.

Goddessdamn me, I had months left of this. But as long as I left everything well taken care of, I could do what needed to be done before my...departure.

"Needin' a cuppa tea, Your Majesty?" Cú asked with a quizzical brow.

"No, not today. Thank you."

He nodded slowly as we both continued to stare out into the hillside.

"Needin' some advice on the new marriage, then?"

I chuckled at his insight.

He continued, "Been married thirty-some years now. Took some time, but I can tell ya what took me too long to be a figurin' out."

I sighed heavily. "And what's that?"

He shrugged. "Give her what she wants. If it don't hurt you none, why not? And even if it do hurt ye, ask yourself if she's worth it."

I laughed, turning back to the grove of trees in the distance. "If I gave her what she's wanted for the past three days, she'd be visiting farms with me."

"Wouldn't hurt no one, would it?" he asked. "When I married Caoimhe, I told her 'no' often enough. Wasn't 'til I realized I was foolin' my own self that I put her first. And she gave me the best somethin' in return."

"And what was that?"

He patted my shoulder. "All of the love she's got. Now I can't live without it, and she just keeps on givin' it."

I glanced south where the castle sat with Morella inside somewhere, listening to a man who was not her husband give her yet another tour of the castle's extensive rooms that no one occupied.

I really was out of excuses.

"Thank you, Cú. I'll consider your words. Until next month."
I nodded my goodbye, headed north to the next farm instead of
south where I felt I should be.

CHAPTER 13

Morella

"I swear to the Goddesses of the Veil, if I have to tour one more sitting room, I'm going to scream."

Fedir huffed and gestured around the seventh hall we'd been to in the last four hours. "I don't know what to tell you, Queen Morella. Castles have a lot of sitting rooms."

I puffed a breath and chewed my lip. "Let's go back to the wool dying vats you showed me yesterday. I'd love to hear more about the flowers they use for color. And I've told you at least ten times—just call me Morella."

"And risk your husband overhearing? Not likely," Fedir said, sinking down into a saffron chair and folding his fingers at his chest.

"As if he'd care," I mumbled, remembering that morning when I'd seen him for a whole five minutes at breakfast before he excused himself again.

"He'd care."

I scoffed, rolling my eyes. "What makes you think he'd care? There's no evidence he cares at all." I gestured around the empty room. "In fact, he's the opposite of caring. He's completely apathetic to his wife's wanderings *four days* into our marriage. If he cared, he'd have made an effort to see me for more than an hour since we wed."

Fedir rubbed the stubble on his chin with golden fingers. "What do you know about Killian and why a Forestfae is king in the land of the Changelingfae?"

Taken aback at the question, I fell into the oversized couch of pale blue satin. This particular sitting room hosted another large fireplace, another writing desk, another shelf of books in a language I didn't know, and another large window looking north to the emerald hillsides dotted with little white sheep.

"I know he was born in Moonstone Wood," I answered slowly. "I know he became king of the Citrine Cliffs at just twenty-two, and I know that just a few months after he took the throne, he bargained with my mother for my hand in marriage."

"Interesting," Fedir muttered, pulling on his chair to sit across from me. "This was all you knew and yet you still came?"

I gestured to myself and the delicate crown Alista insisted I wear, frustrated at how badly this whole marriage had gone so far. "Obviously."

He sat back with a light chuckle. "Here's what I can tell you because *obviously*, you're dying to know."

I shifted slightly, crossing my own arms and trying not to look too eager for any little sliver of information about the man I'd married, whose magic I desperately needed.

"King Killian ascended the throne as was ordained by Céad, Goddess of the Changelingfae. As I'm sure you are well aware, she has no children—no heir—and set out to find one about thirteen years ago."

Oh, fuck. This was real information. Real history of my husband's life.

Grinning at my not-so-subtle reaction, he continued, "Killian had immense power among the Forestfae. Enough so that Fiola told Céad he would make a great king and very possibly, a greater heir."

"Can an heir to a Goddess be of a different faekind?"

"No."

We both jumped, turning to the voice in the doorway. Killian glared furiously at Fedir who stood and sauntered toward the door.

"Just filling in some gaps during the tour," he said with a shrug.

"You needn't," Killian responded curtly.

"Are you still so sure about that, Your Majesty?" Fedir jerked his head in my direction where I straightened on the sofa. He patted my husband's shoulder and left without another word.

I rose and met Killian at the doorway, accepting my body's reaction to seeing him there, commanding space with his red waves tied back and eyes of sparkling blue watching me carefully.

"Hello, husband," I greeted, just inches from him. "How fare the farms?"

His stoney stare held mine in a challenge to look away.

Well, I wasn't fucking going to.

"Fine," he finally said. "And how fares the castle?"

Matching his response with a playful lilt, I repeated, "Fine."

"You've seen it all, then?"

I thought for a moment, my mind wandering through the many halls, rooms, and courtyards. "The westward tower," I blurted. "I've not seen it yet."

His brows furrowed as if he wrestled with his next words. "Would you like to?"

"Yes!" I answered, beaming at his offer.

A ghost of a smile graced his lips and he turned, jerking his head in the tower's direction.

Giddy with hope, I followed, catching up to his side and biting my tongue from asking all the questions I wanted answered.

What exactly entailed checking on the farms?

Were there any problems to address?

What was his favorite book in the castle?

What would his beard feel like against the skin on my thigh?

Goddessdamn me, I just wanted to know.

What did it feel like, being ravished by a man who actually knew what he was doing?

Something told me Killian would know exactly what he was doing.

And then I'd be fucked in more ways than one.

If my husband didn't intend to have such a relationship with me, the last thing I needed was to have him just once or twice and forever remember what that was like.

Focus, Morella, focus.

"I know what you're thinking," he murmured softly as we rounded a corner.

"Y-you do?"

"You're thinking you've made a mistake."

Wrong.

"You're thinking that this castle is not for you. This king you married is not for you."

Wrong and more wrong.

We approached an arched doorway leading to worn stone stairs that wound upwards, disappearing into the tower. He took a candle from the lit sconce and led our ascent. "You're thinking that the three month amendment to our contract is looking more and more like a Goddessblessing and a way out of this marriage."

He fell into silence. The only sound was the flickering of the small flame and our footsteps up the stone spiral. We soon came to a small landing and old wooden door that I doubted saw much use.

Trying not to puff my breath from climbing the stairs, I finally spoke. "None of those things have crossed my mind."

Frowning, he pulled a long copper key from his pocket. Sliding it into the keyhole, the mechanism clicked and the door hinged inward in a resounding groan. He offered me the candle and I took it, stepping into the dark room that boasted a single sliver of an open window facing west. The lowering sun gilded the room in a dim orange glow. Stepping further into the tower room, I held the candle aloft, lighting another covered in dust along the stone wall. He stepped in behind me and shut the door.

The room didn't hold much. In fact, it appeared to be used more as storage than anything. A few trinkets lay in an old trunk and some wooden chairs were stacked near the door. A bed of straw lay under the window and an old spinning wheel was laced with cobwebs nearby.

"Why didn't you break the contract?"

The question filtered through the small circular room, still unanswered from the first time he'd asked it.

I turned to face him. "I told you. I didn't want to."

His mask of stone wavered. "What do you want from me, Morella?" he asked slowly.

Everything.

All of it.

All of you.

"Is it so hard to believe I *want* to be your wife? Why do you resist this marriage every step of the way?"

"Because from what I've observed, you're intelligent. Intelligent women don't show up in a foreign kingdom after thirteen years and marry a foreign king unless they have a goal in mind."

Well, shit. He had me there.

I stepped closer, drawn to his voice. "Did you just compliment me again? That makes a miraculous *two* times."

"You're counting?"

"On one hand."

He laughed, shaking his head. Folding his arms at his chest and drawing my eye to his considerable biceps, he continued, "Alright. I'll play along until I find the real reason you're here.

You *want* to be queen? What do you have to offer the Changlingfae as their ruler?"

"Well..." I began, "I'm intelligent, as you said—"

"Yes, we've covered that."

"And," I replied with a smirk, "I'm knowledgeable in your trade."

"Which is?"

"Wool. Fine clothing. Fedir gave me a tour of the fabric stores underneath the castle and the vats of dye. This kingdom is known for its wool production, and offering the softest, yet pliable wool in all of Revelry."

Again that almost smile hinted on his lips. "And how are you knowledgeable in wool production?"

"Well, I...I am a very good spinner."

He quirked a brow and I felt the need to go on. "I mean to say, my spinning is accurate and quick."

His silence continued.

"I-I can spin anything, really."

"Anything?" he repeated with a tilt of his head.

"I'm sure I could."

I thought of the goats I had sheared one year, spinning their long coats and of the mohari beast who had lost his way in the Brackish Wood. His fibers had made Korven a fine scarf that winter.

"Could you spin straw?" he asked with a shrug.

Taken aback, I huffed quickly, "It's likely I could."

A slow smile spread on his lips. "There is straw here, Morella. There is a spinning wheel."

"Oh," I murmured, turning to see that those exact two things were indeed there in that tower room, waiting for me to prove myself.

"Well, I don't know if this spinning wheel is in the right shape to—"

"Humor me."

I peered at him over my shoulder. This was his test. Fuck, if I'd fail it.

Approaching the spinning wheel, I shoved my sleeves up my arms, inspecting each moving part. The wheel turned with ease and the bobbin was intact, albeit covered in dust. I blew away as much as I could and sat at the stool, pumping at the treadle and adjusting the maidens to my liking.

My husband watched me with rapt curiosity, likely expecting me to come up with more excuses for why it was impossible to spin straw.

Spin straw into *what*?

I rose and pulled at the straw bed, examining the long, dry pieces. Though they were dusty, they were pliable—enough so to tie together. I sat at the stool and got to work, taking the longer pieces and tying them at the ends in a simple knot. Once I had a string of them, I began to wind the bobbin, just as I would have done with wool.

Questioning my own sanity, I checked the tension in the maidens, pulling the long string of tied straw into my hand with another bundle ready. I glanced up at the window, ignoring the man who'd challenged me and ignited my Goddessdamn stubbornness, born and bred into me as a Ravenfae.

The sun sat lower now, spreading soft rays through the narrow slit. Fresh, sweet air drifted through the open window, a hint at the autumn to come. I took a deep breath, pinched the straw between my fingers, and began treadling.

The amber light reminded me of gold.

The gold of my wings.

The gold of the trinkets around our room.

The gold in the flecks of my eyes and the gold undertone of my husband's skin. The copper in his hair shone in that lowering light, reflecting in bright sparks of golden waves that framed his face in light flyaways.

My husband had never said it, but I believed gold just might be his favorite.

As the footman drove the wheel, I imagined that the straw was a line of thread, winding around the bobbin as a gift to the man I wanted to know and the man I needed to save my brother's wife.

I felt the straw shift in my hands as it ran through my forefinger and thumb, twisting and glimmering into strands of the purest golden thread I'd ever seen. Fascinated, I kept the treadle running as smoothly as possible, enjoying the rhythmic turning of the wheel I'd spent most of my life perfecting.

My body warmed and my chest swelled as the bobbin continued to spin, woven strands of gold threading tightly around its base. As the straw grew sparse in my hand, I slowed the treadle, rising to release the bobbin. I pressed the thread with my fingers, inspecting for tightness of the weave and quality.

Without a word, I held out the bobbin, allowing my husband to see exactly what talents I could bring to this kingdom as its queen.

He pulled on the thread, taking a moment to inspect it himself. His frown deepened. "Who was your father?"

Consistently surprised by his questions, I answered with a bemused, "Huh?"

"Your father, Morella," he repeated. "Do you know him?"

"No."

"Your brother—does he share your golden wings?"

I cocked my head. "No."

"You have different fathers, then?"

"Yes—what are these questions about? I thought you'd be happy to find that your queen can spin straw into golden thread."

"Begging for another compliment?" he asked, peering down at me with those sapphire eyes again.

"Yes!" I admitted, snatching the bobbin from his hand and

unwinding some of the thread. "Name another who could spin as well as I can!"

He shook his head. "There is no other. I'd bet this kingdom that you are the only fae alive who could do such a thing. Do you know why Citrine Wool is so widely sought after in Revelry?"

"Of course I do. I work with it often. The fibers are soft and rarely show signs of breakage. The wool does not shrink and hardly needs combing." I shrugged, knowing he already knew all of this. "It keeps you warm in winter and cool in summer."

"Exactly," he agreed. His lips upturned in the first real smile I'd seen. "Our sheep produce the finest wool in Revelry, but have you ever stopped to question why?"

"Of course, I have. It must be the grass or something."

"Or something." He took the bundled thread from my hands, holding up the long strand to the window to watch the thread glisten.

"It's not the grass?"

"No," he answered in a wry smile. "It's moss."

"Moss?"

"From the Brackish Wood."

I shook my head, stumbling in my thoughts. It couldn't be... could it? Surely not... surely I wasn't bargained for...

"You catch on quickly," he laughed.

"You—you're saying you bargained for my hand in marriage with moss?"

"An entire crop with direct instructions on how we could grow it here ourselves. We couldn't rely on the Brackish Wood forever. I had your mother throw in a few different types of mushrooms as well, but the sheep weren't interested."

"*Reshina*," I corrected, "the Ravenfae *Goddess* would not have contracted my marriage over a clump of dirty spores."

"And the mushrooms," he added, suppressing his chuckle.

"This isn't fucking funny, Killian!"

He caught my shoulders, shaking me. "I'll pity you when you

tell me why you stayed. I negotiated this marriage for moss, yes, but I also gave you the opportunity to get out of it." His hands shifted down my arms. "Trivially."

"Fine," I started, stepping out of his reach and raising my chin. "I need you."

"How so?"

"Your power to change things."

"There it is." He folded his arms. "Go on. What exactly do you need to change?"

"I'd heard of you. I knew you could...could manipulate things and make them different from what they once were."

He listened in silence, his face still as stone.

"At first I accepted because I thought you could help my mother with her curse...but Korven taught me she'd have to break that herself—if she ever does."

He nodded once.

"Then," I continued, "I considered breaking the contract. That was until I met Seraphine."

"Who is Seraphine?"

Annoyed he didn't already know, I explained. "She is my brother's wife." I gulped, meeting his eyes. "And she is human."

"Ah," he breathed. "You need me to change Seraphine into faekind."

I stepped forward, my heart racing. *Please, please, please.* "I need you to change Seraphine into faekind."

He rubbed his chin, his eyes staring over my head for a few moments. "I'd like to offer you a bargain, Goldling."

Pretending I didn't just shiver at this new nickname, I forced my face into something altogether unfazed. "I'm listening."

"Discover my true name and I will change your Seraphine. She will live long with your brother and dying well before him will cease to be anyone's fear. Including yours."

My face contorted in confusion. "Discover your...what? What does that even mean?"

"I cannot help you further."

"Well, fuck, Killian! What kind of bargain is that?"

"The only one that will save your brother's wife from an early grave."

I shoved him. Hard. Built like a marble statue, he barely moved and now I was in his space where he caught my hands at his chest, pressing my wrists together.

"You will receive no other explanation from me. And just for that,"—he squeezed my hands at his chest—"I'm adding on to the deal. You will also spin three spools of golden thread each day for the last three months left in this marriage."

"Last three..."

"*And*,"—he squeezed again—"You will take lessons in Céaduah, the language of the Changelingfae."

Oh, *Goddess fucking damn him.*

I wrestled my wrists from his grasp and stumbled, almost tripping on the spinning wheel. He caught me at the small of my back, lifting me upright as if he'd dipped me in a dance.

I pressed myself to his chest with my whole body. "If you get to add onto our deal, so do I." I gripped his jacket. "*You* will be teaching me Céaduah."

"I do not have the time to—"

"Find time," I snapped. "*And*,"—I rose onto the tips of my toes to meet his face with mine—"You will kiss me goodnight every night as if we are actually married."

"That's two amendments."

"You added two."

"One was just for pushing me."

"My second is for that Goddess-awful kiss you gave me at our wedding."

"You didn't enjoy my lips pressed to yours, Goldling?"

"One of the many disappointments of the day."

His hand at my back pulled me closer, his lips so near to mine, I felt the warmth of his breath. His eyes darted to my mouth and my lips parted. I knew if he kissed me now, I'd melt in his arms because I wanted him. My whole body wanted all of him and didn't seem to care how much my mind wanted nothing more than to push him down the stairs and toss his precious golden thread behind him.

He met my gaze again, a grin blooming across his mouth. "Deal," he whispered between us.

I closed my mouth and swallowed hard, straightening my spine in his hands. "Deal."

His lips met mine in a searing kiss, sharp and wild as he opened his mouth, pulling my bottom lip into his. He let go, his hand holding up my chin with an utterly wicked smile across his face and a challenge in his eyes.

"That didn't count," I said quickly.

"That one was free."

He let go of me entirely, turning his back. "The sun sets. I suggest you get to work before the day is through and you've broken the bargain already."

"You want me to spin three cops of gold *today*?"

"Do you want me to kiss you tonight?"

I huffed, folding my arms. "Not really."

"Too bad." He waved a hand behind him and walked out the door, calling, "Meet me in our room for your first lesson when you're finished. And don't be too late."

FEDIR ENTERED MY STUDY AS I PINCHED THE GOLDEN
thread, inspecting the spin, the tightness, the strength—it had
been nothing short of pure Changlingfae magic that Morella was
able to transmute straw into gold.

"How was the rest of the tour?" my captain teased, tossing
himself into an armchair by the fire.

"She can spin straw into this." I chucked the spool of thread
into the air where Fedir caught it.

He frowned but chuckled. "Odd joke, but I'll play along.
What do you mean by straw?"

Rising from my desk, I joined him by the fire. "What I mean
is that the Queen of the Citrine Cliffs took a handful of straw
and spun it on a spinning wheel into *that*."

He shook his head, pulling on the thread and winding it
around his hand. "We assumed she must have Changlingfae
blood, but something like this is..."

"*Exactly.*" I leaned back in my seat, staring at the low
flames.

His chest rumbled and he set the thread down, crossing his
leg over his knee and settling back. "She's definitely under your
skin. Didn't expect that, did you?"

"Of course I didn't," I snapped. "She was supposed to be dull, ugly, and simple. Just as you predicted she would be."

He tsked. "I can't be correct all the time, Your Majesty."

"You were supposed to be right about *her*. Your ability to predict the change is the reason I keep you around."

"Sure, sure," he laughed. "Changelingfae magic doesn't always work the same way twice. You know that. Hence the *change* part. And to be fair, I did predict the change in *you*. I said you would soften your heart to your future wife."

"There was no softening. I wanted to throw her over my shoulder and take her to bed the moment I locked eyes on her, and then toss her out to go find someone else to marry who could actually love her."

"Ah. I see I should have said you'd *harden* to her, then."

"*Fedir,*" I scolded. But he was right, and we both knew it.

I rubbed my face, shifting my fingers through my beard. "I offered her the bargain."

He almost tumbled out of his chair. "Thank the Goddess," he breathed, slipping to the edge of his seat. "Did she take it?"

"Yes," I huffed a laugh despite myself, remembering her face as it lit in the challenge. "I added a few amendments...as did she."

He smiled slyly. "Amendments?"

"The only ones you need to know are that I will be teaching her Céaduah. And she'll be spinning more of this each day." I pointed to the golden thread.

"The wheel of change is spinning fast, my friend. You cannot slip up. This is your—"

"Last chance," I finished. "I know."

"Three months," he sighed, rising from his seat and taking the thread with him.

He knew what to do with it. They'd want it in the vaults below the castle. We dyed our threads gold, but this...this would raise a fortune if the weavers could use it in their embroidering.

Real threaded gold.

"Three months," I repeated. "It has to be enough time for her to discover my name."

"For her?" he said, tossing the spool of thread into the air on his way out the door. "I think so. But for you to make it that long?" He caught the spool in his golden fingers. "That I'm less sure about."

He shut the door on his way out, leaving me with the same fear.

Regardless, I had no choice.

My fate was now tied to the Golden Queen of the Citrine Cliffs.

CHAPTER 15

Morella

I WAS GOING TO *MAIM* MY HUSBAND.

Fingers raw and stiff, I chucked the third bobbin of shimmering thread across the tower room where it hit the open door, unspooling across the stone.

"Shit fucking dammit!" I hollered, bolting from my wooden stool to catch the thread before it completely unwound down the stairs.

"Queen Morella?" The voice lingered somewhere below in the stairwell.

"I'm up here!" I called, slumping onto the first step and quickly winding the thread, ready to leave this tower for the night...until tomorrow.

Alista's head of golden ringlets appeared before me as I sat with three spools of golden thread in my lap and a yawn I covered with the back of my hand.

"Your Majesty!" she cried, gathering her skirts and racing up the steps. "I've been searching for you! Why in the name of the Goddess are you up here?"

I rubbed my eyes, silently handing her a bobbin. "You didn't ask my dear husband where he sequestered me to?"

"King Killian has locked himself away in his study, not to be disturbed."

"Well," I began, standing and stretching, handing her the rest of the thread. "Before that we made a bargain which included these. Please take them down to the workers in clothing production so they can do something useful with them."

She studied the spools, pulling on the thread. "Your Majesty... is this..."

"Golden thread, yes," I finished.

"Real gold, my queen?"

"Yes, spun from straw."

She gasped, clutching the spools to her chest. "Then you *are* a Changelingfae!" She laughed, the sound tinkling and echoing down the stairwell. "I'd heard the rumors because of your golden wings, but I wasn't so sure myself and then Captain Fedir insisted he saw you as a golden raven when you arrived at the—"

"Wait, go back." I held up my hands, catching her eyes. "You're telling me I'm a Changelingfae?"

She cocked her head with a sly smile. "You didn't know? The gold tips of your wings is one thing, but your power to transform an object into another confirms it."

I glanced at her golden curls. "So, you're a Changelingfae as well? Do...do we all have gold on our bodies?"

"Yes!" she exclaimed happily. "Yes, every Changelingfae is marked by gold, just as every Ravenfae is marked by feathered wings, correct?"

I nodded, understanding Killian's questioning about my father.

Changelingfae.

I had no idea. My whole life, I hadn't met another one. Did my mother know my father was? Did Korven know *what* I was?

"Excuse me, Alista, I must get back to my room."

She curtsied as I passed her down the stairs. "Of course, Your

Majesty! Please call for me if you need assistance undressing tonight!"

"I won't, but thank you!" I called back, rushing down the lit halls in a half-run to get to my husband who had some questions to answer.

I burst through our ornately carved bedroom door, making a mental note to study the scenes depicted in the artistry later. "Killian!" I called, searching the room to find it empty. I quickly knocked on his study door, hardly pausing before he bid me to enter.

I rushed through, finding myself in a small chamber complete with a large desk and two chairs sharing a small table next to a fireplace. The rest of the room was lined with immaculately shelved books along every wall, floor to ceiling. It must have been over a thousand volumes.

"Is this the castle library?" I asked, distracted and pulling a thick volume from the shelf labeled, *Grasses and Their Phosphorus Levels*. Opening the book, I found it filled with regions of Revelry and charts for soil minerals.

"Lebher," he replied, rising from his desk to join me.

"Sorry?" I looked up from the detailed notes scribbled on the margins of the book.

He tapped the old tome and repeated, "Lebher." Then he pointed to the door behind me, adding, "Doru."

"Oh..." Apparently, my lessons in Céaduah had begun. I closed the book and repeated, "Leb-*hair*."

He held in a smile, shaking his head and spoke slowly, "Leb-*her*."

"Leb*her*," I repeated, adding the guttural sound with the back of my throat.

"Good, Morella."

I blushed furiously, ticking another compliment onto my hand, albeit a small one.

Noticing my reddened cheeks, he held up four fingers with a raised brow.

Ignoring him, I pointed to the door, repeating, "Doru."

He nodded, taking the book from me and placing it tidily back into its spot. "Where are your spools of thread?"

"With Alista. I asked her to take them below to the workrooms."

He smirked thoughtfully. "Time for your first lesson then, Goldling." He gestured to the chairs by the fire and I took one, settling myself by slipping off my shoes and tucking my feet underneath me. I was no longer tired. I was no longer frustrated with my task of spinning straw into golden thread. Instead, I was enraptured. My husband sat opposite, taking up all the space in the room, let alone the actual chair. He leaned forward on his legs, built like trunks of trees. A shiver ran through me at his undivided attention.

"Ta fìor lebherahlann a' casteil on ùir ann uamh," he said.

I scrunched my nose. "Don't you think that's a bit too advanced for me?"

"I want you to hear Céaduah often. Really let it settle in here." He tapped his chest over his heart. "The servants will begin to add it to their speech when addressing you. You'll pick up on it quicker that way."

I cocked my head to the side, mimicking the look I'd seen my brother pose a thousand times. "Were you always planning to teach me Céaduah?"

He rubbed his scruffy chin. "No."

"You decided this today," I stated.

A twitch of his lips. "Yes."

"After you saw proof that I am part Changelingfae."

"Ah, so you've figured that out."

"No, I was *told*. And not by my husband, as I should have been."

He shrugged. "As I said, you are an intelligent woman,

Goldling. You'd have discovered it on your own eventually." Something sat on his face and he leaned back in his chair, folding his hands at his chest.

I studied his features. This man held many secrets—that I could see—but which were the ones I needed to get what I wanted from him?

"Is Céaduah necessary to know as a ruler of the Citrine Cliffs?" I muttered, my mind spinning.

His face remained still as he answered with a short shake of his head.

"You didn't plan to teach me, yet when you began our bargain, you added this as an amendment. You cannot tell me your true name; I must discover it for myself."

His eyes filled with something I couldn't name. Something I'd seen twice on his face. Once when he first laid eyes on me arriving at our wedding on the arm of Fedir. And once more after I'd spun the first golden thread.

"You're almost there," he murmured, waiting in the silence.

I straightened in my chair with a wide grin. "Your true name *means* something in Céaduah. You need me to learn the language to discover it."

"There it is, Moh Dhóches."

"What's...moh dhóches?"

"You'll have to learn."

I huffed, glancing at the fire. "Earlier, what did you say after you sat down? Lebherahlann something something. If lebher means book, what is *lebherahlann*?"

"Impressive, Morella. You have a gift for language."

I bit my lip at compliment number five.

He continued, "'Lebherahlann means library. I was answering your previous question as to if this room is the castle library. It's not."

"Repeat your answer, please."

"*Ta fîor lebherahlann a' casteil on ùir ann uamh.*"

"The something library..." I repeated the sentence over and over in my head, searching for similar patterns to the common language in Revelry. "Is *casteil* castle?"

His eyes lit with amusement. "It is."

I nodded, thinking hard and mumbling to myself. "Give me another meaning. What is *ùir*?"

"Soil or ground in this case."

"The castle library is in the ground?" I attempted.

He laughed in a rich, carefree tenor. "Well done!" He stood, jerking his head toward the door that led to our room. "'Ta fìor lebherahlann a' casteil on ùir ann uamh.' In common, 'The true castle library is below the ground in a cave.'"

"A cave?" I gasped, following him into our room.

"*Ann uamh.*"

"Will you take me there?" I asked, reaching behind my back to untie my gown. His hand grabbed my fingers and I turned in surprise.

His eyes narrowed and he let go. "Don't undress in front of me." He jerked his head to the screen panels hiding my bed. "I've given you a place for privacy."

Gulping and nodding, I shuffled behind the screen, hidden from my husband and conflicted with how to feel about him. Did he send me behind the screen so I wouldn't get the wrong idea of his intentions? Or did he send me behind the screen because he didn't want to admit how my undressing would make him react? Because it didn't feel like he didn't want me. It didn't feel like his eyes darkened on my figure for any reason other than exactly that.

I undressed quickly, stepping into my crimson nightgown and slipped out from the screen, hurrying to the bathing room without another word. My teeth clean and my face washed, I plaited my hair into a tidy length that fell over my shoulder and slipped back through the door, practically jumping into my bed and pulling the soft covers up over my body.

I was too nervous to ask for a kiss goodnight.

And far too tired to argue about it.

For now, in the dim glow of the last candle lit in the room, I felt foolish for ever bringing it up at all. The relationship I wanted with my husband was one he seemed determined to resist, so who was I to pressure him?

I closed my eyes and pretended to sleep as he left the bathing chamber. The side of my bed creaked with the weight of him and my eyes flew open, finding his face in shadow with the last glow of the candle at his bedside behind him, illuminating the red of his hair.

"Ann pìor, Morella."

My eyes drifted to his lips. I could guess what that meant.

I sat up, nodding. "Ann pìor, Killian."

He leaned in to kiss me, this time softer, this time gentle and slow, sending my racing heart into a fit of want and need. I gripped the bedding in my fists, never touching him, never grabbing onto his bare shoulders and pulling him down onto me where I wanted him. As our lips parted and he sat back, I tried to guess if it was what he wanted, too.

"Goodnight, Moh Dhóches," he whispered.

"Goodnight," I repeated, slipping back into my sheets, trembling with excitement, and fear, and lust for my husband who slid into his own bed and blew out the last flicker of light.

CHAPTER 16

Killian

I WASN'T SURE HOW LONG I LAID THERE.

Long enough to pick up the steady ease of her breathing.

Long enough to settle my body, restless as it had been.

Long enough to hear her hum and turn in her bed.

Long enough to pray to every Goddess in Revelry that I was strong enough to resist moh dhóches.

Long enough to convince myself to close my eyes and attempt to rest when the feel of her lips pressed to mine was the only thing that was ever going to get me through each day to each night from now until the end.

I'D BEEN TRAPPED IN MY NIGHTMARES FOR YEARS NOW.

Each night, the sweat and fear.

Each morning, the reassurance in the mirror that I still had time.

Some mornings it was hope.

Some it was nothing more than the constant reminder that I

would leave my kingdom a more prosperous one than I'd found it.

That morning, I gripped the sides of the porcelain sink, breathing deep through my nose, exhaling long through my mouth. Sweat dripped from my nose into the basin and my eyes watered at the thought...

But their deaths were fifteen years ago, and I had grown into a different man since then. A different king.

I didn't need the same things now that I had needed many years before.

Our beds were separate.

Our time together would be brief.

And with whatever Goddessblessed luck I had left, the clever queen would discover my true name in her studies and free me from this torment.

I washed my face and shaved away the overgrown gruff on my face and neck. When I finished, I slid into the bath that was always left for me in the early hours of dawn. I had a servant fill the tub every night and by morning, I could calm myself in the cold water.

The sun would rise in another hour and another day would begin.

Another day of work.

Another day of hope.

Another day closer to the end, one way or another.

CHAPTER 17

Morella

FOR THE SECOND WEEK OF OUR MARRIAGE, KILLIAN AND I spent most of our days apart, as seemed to be normal for us. He carried on with business in the mornings, and I spent time spinning straw and visiting the weavers who were in awe of what I brought them each day. I received his lessons each night along with his kiss goodnight—each one not much more than a simple peck on the lips. I threw off how tired I was, rationing my thistle nuts as best I could, and finally sat down to write to my family.

> Dearest Korven, Seraphine, and little Avici,
> I miss you all! I have been married for two weeks now, and my new husband and I are adjusting to each other. The castle is beautiful and large—complete with four standing towers and an underground library I have yet to visit.
> Everyone has been so kind and welcoming, and I think it will just take some time for me to really find my place here.

Korven, please reply with a detailed explanation of how in the fuck I am part Changelingfae. Did you even know?

I miss all three of you.

All my love,

Morella

P.S. thistle nuts

I FOLDED THE LETTER AND PLACED IT INTO THE THICK brown envelope, sealing it with gold wax and a stamp depicting a fat mushroom. I reached into my pocket for another thistle nut, chewing absentmindedly as Alista knocked and entered our room.

"Please send this off, Alista."

She nodded, taking the letter. "Anything else, my queen? Our washing maids have almost all of that blue ointment out of your gowns and they should finish today." She eyed my open trunk which spilled with the rest of my clothes. "Would you like me to unpack this for you?"

"No, thank you. I'd like to spend the morning getting to that myself."

She nodded and took my breakfast tray, frowning. "Do you not enjoy fuilhe, Queen Morella?"

I pulled a gown from my trunk, checking for stains and eyeing the black circle of meat left on my tray. "I'm afraid I do not."

She tsked her tongue. "It is good for you. Good for the blood and good for future children in the womb."

I choked on my spit, hacking into my arm. "Alista, there's no child—I mean, there's no chance of—Because we haven't—"

She cleared her throat, eyeing the two separate beds in the room. "I see."

Embarrassed, I continued my work, pulling out the endless jars and setting each one onto the shelf of my wardrobe, including the jar of tea that would prevent a child for an entire month. Alista bowed quietly and left while I huffed, wondering if it mattered at all that I'd already taken the tea the night before my wedding.

I shook my head. Either Killian would treat me as his wife in time or he wouldn't at all. For now, I had a job to do and that was discovering his true name and saving my sister.

I stacked a few more jars and hung the three gowns I had left —one yellow, one red, and one blue. The gown I wore was a deep green, the color of a dark pine in winter. I popped another thistle nut into my mouth and took a deep breath. My wings felt heavy at my back and my eyes threatened to droop with exhaustion.

I finished unpacking and knocked on Killian's study door.

"You may enter if you can ask to enter in Céaduah," he called.

A smirk threatened on my lips as I leaned in. "Am faodre mi dub a stuh?"

"Enter," he replied.

I stepped through to see him writing in a ledger. The window behind his desk was open to the waning summer air and the bustle of castle life could be heard in distant voices. I clasped my hands behind my back and perused the bookshelves, tilting my head and munching on thistle nuts as I read each title.

The Art of Wool

A Detailed History of Shepherding

Wool Carding and Combing

That book I tugged from its placement and opened to the middle, scanning the hand-drawn diagrams and reading the captions.

"Do you read often?"

His voice came sudden and deep and I jumped slightly, choking on a nut. I turned to him, closing the book. "Not nearly as often as Seraphine, so I don't know what 'often' means to any one person."

He stopped his writing and looked up to meet my eyes with his. "Let me rephrase. Do you *enjoy* reading, Morella?"

I'd enjoy reading to *him*. I'd enjoy reading near him, under him, over him—"*Stop it*," I muttered under my breath.

"What?"

"I do." I snapped the book shut, shelving it quickly.

His gaze flicked over my dress, my braided hair, and my wings which had shifted outward at my last thoughts.

Returning to his ledger, he instructed, "You'll find fresh straw in the stables for your task this morning."

I huffed, slumping into the chair in front of his desk, popping another nut from my pocket and chewing slowly. "How am I to get the straw up to the tower?"

"Can you not shift with it? I imagine a raven could easily fit through the tower window and my understanding is that Ravenfae shift with whatever they carry or wear."

"Can you shift through wood like other Forestfae?" I asked, crossing my legs and adjusting my wings.

"Yes," he grumbled, continuing his work.

"Can you shift with things? Heavy things?"

"Yes, Morella."

"Is that how you got my bed and wardrobe into our room so easily? You're quite strong. I bet you could maneuver both on your own."

"Your assessment of my strength is cor—what are you eating?" He finally looked my way again as I nibbled on another nut absentmindedly.

I swallowed my mouthful. "They're thistle nuts. I eat them throughout the day." I pulled one from my pocket, holding it out in an offering. "Would you like one? They only grow in the Brackish Wood that I know of."

Reaching across the desk and taking the nut from my outstretched hand, he eyed it in curiosity before biting off a corner.

I tossed the rest of my small handful into my mouth, enjoying the confusion on his face.

"You eat these everyday?"

Nodding, I replied, "If I don't eat enough, I tend to succumb to exhaustion."

He chewed the rest, eyeing me with caution.

I dusted my hands and swept crumbs from my dress. "Well," I started, standing awkwardly, "if you need me, you know where I'll be for the next hour or two."

He began writing again. "I won't need you."

Well, fuck. Our second week was going swimmingly.

"You really don't have to do that, you know," I burst before I could rethink what I wanted to say.

"Do what?" he asked, barely acknowledging me.

"Dismiss me so trivially."

He tossed his quill into the pot of ink and slammed his book shut with a thud. Rising from his chair, he darted around his desk, flexing his hands before slipping them into his pockets. He jerked his head towards the door as he passed me, with the simple instruction of, "Come."

With the excitement of whatever this was, I followed him like a lost puppy, practically running to keep up with his heavy foot-fall across the gilded halls of our castle. Nodding to each servant and guard we passed, he didn't say a word, nor did he slow his pace as I huffed behind him, begging him to slow down. He had at least ten inches on me and his legs were long, massive things as he strode down the halls and stairwells without so much as a misplaced breath.

I lost track of our way at stairwell number six and completely bumped into his enormous back as he stopped abruptly at a door in a dark stone hall. He turned just in time to catch my wrist before I fell on my ass and embarrassed myself further.

"Count to one hundred and then follow me down these stairs."

Frowning, I nodded as he opened the door and descended into the dark. I peeked after him and began counting in my head, but beyond the first few steps, I couldn't see a thing.

I had the feeling I knew exactly where he was leading me, but why now, why right as I let my mouth run away with me, I couldn't guess.

As I reached ninety-nine, I was already several steps down, following the pale golden glow that had lit up the stairs around number seventy-two.

This staircase wound around a center pillar like the western tower, and as I cautiously took each step, the light became more insistent and my heart beat in frantic curiosity.

At last, I found the last few steps and gasped in absolute awe of the true library of the castle. Pillars of translucent golden citrine, pure and tower in shape, erupted from the cavern walls like growths of divine light. Varying in size, each held a glow within, illuminating the books tucked into the cavern walls as far as my eyes could see. I stepped further into the tunnel, near to tears and overcome with the glorious underground library.

Killian watched in silence as I trailed my fingers across a crystal larger than me before finding my way to a shelf carved into the walls.

"The books you're looking for are here," he called softly, his voice echoing in the cavern. He gestured to a few rows of books with red leather casings. I pulled one from the shelf and read, "Céaduah, Language of the Changelingfae, Volume four." Meeting his eyes, I asked, "How many volumes are there?"

"Thirteen."

Holding back a shiver, I replaced volume four, pulling volumes one and two instead.

"Follow this tunnel. There's more you need to see."

I did exactly as he said, shuffling through the tunnel which narrowed as I walked, still providing thousands of books in varying subjects. Some I could see were written in Céaduah and I wondered just how much history of the Changelingfae people was hidden underneath their kingdom's castle.

I must have voiced that last part out loud, because he answered with a low grumble. "Some of these books date all the way back to Céad's arrival on Revelry from the Veil."

I turned to him, pressing the two books tightly to my chest. "Can I come here whenever I'd like?"

He nodded, stepping closer, the amber glow of the crystals illuminating the red of his hair and casting a golden glow over his clean-shaven face. I allowed myself to stare. He did the same as we studied each other in the soft light.

Down here, we were just two people who had met two weeks ago.

Down here, we were teacher and student.

Down here, there was no bargain or pressure on the both of us to come together in marriage. Down here it was just him. It was just me.

I stepped forward and held out my hand between us. "If we had met any other way, I would have wanted to know you."

Something ticked in his jaw and his face hardened.

I continued, pushing out my hand further. "My name is Morella. It's nice to meet you, Killian."

He laughed, relaxing his shoulders and slid his hand in mine. "Morella," he spoke in a low voice, smooth as silk. "It's nice to meet you, too."

CHAPTER 18

Killian

GOLD-TIPPED WINGS.

A penchant for speaking her mind.

A cleverness I'd still not seen the full depths of.

A dark red dress that I'd married her in.

A talent for spinning straw into gold—this woman had cut through more than I'd let her know.

And following her now through the citrine library, I felt that burst of hope I hadn't allowed in a decade.

The morning light brightened her way and she stepped out of the crystal tunnel, clutching her books to her chest. She shielded the sun from her eyes and gasped at the sight.

The Citrine Cliffs lived up to their name. We stood on a sharp precipice overlooking a vast escarpment, long and narrow in the valley below. The natural amber crystals jutted from the steep plateaus and reflected in the morning sun, glinting light that pirouetted through the cliffside.

"Killian…" she started, her eyes bright, her mouth agape, "it's incredible!" She laughed and placed her hand on my forearm, just as she'd done that morning after our wedding. "Thank you."

Her eyes filled with the golden light of a happiness I'd not felt in years.

"Do you see that grove of trees there?" I pointed across the expanse of land below us to a small crop of trees growing across the canyon.

She nodded and I continued. "Can you meet me there? There's something else I need to show you."

Her face fell, but she recovered quickly and nodded again. I took my place at the gnarled tree growing along the side of our cliff and shifted through the wood, sifting through many trees until I walked through the one I needed at the cliffside.

I could see her form in contrast to the golden crystals behind her, far across the valley. In truth, I could have shifted through the trees with her wrapped in my arms, but decided against it for two reasons.

One, I wanted to see her golden raven form.

Two, I didn't want to touch her more than necessary.

I walked to the cliff's pointed edge and waved both of my arms up over my head.

She hesitated a few moments more before shifting into a speck of gold in the morning light. Her flight was slow across the sky and more than once she dipped suddenly, her wings wavering and tilted.

I found myself at the very edge, leaning toward her as she dipped again. *She wasn't going to make it.* My heart thundered in my chest and my scream erupted across the valley as she began to fall, twisting in a haze of golden feathers to the forest floor below. I bolted to the nearest tree, calculating each shift until I shot out of the tree line underneath her.

"Morella!" I screamed, lining myself up to catch her.

Her golden raven body fell into my arms and I cradled her to my chest. Her head hung limp and her chest heaved. Alive. She was alive and breathing.

I sifted through the trees, shuffling through them one by one in a matter of seconds before stepping out of our bedroom door in the castle. Still cradling her in my arms, I opened the door and called down the hall. "Get Captain Fedir!"

Rushing to my bed, I laid her raven form gently on my pillow. Her shift was languid as she came back to her Ravenfae form, her eyes closed and still catching her breath, books in hand. "Morella?" I urged, brushing the sweat soaked hair from her brow. "Can you hear me?"

Nodding slightly, she blinked, pulling herself up to sitting. "Water?"

Fedir approached the bed, thrusting a cup into my hands and I held it to her lips.

She swatted my hand lazily, took the cup, and drank. "I almost made it," she mumbled in a short, humorless laugh.

"Why didn't you tell me you couldn't make it across?" I snapped. "I would have taken you had I known—"

"That I'm too weak of a flier to span such a distance?" she finished. "I might have been able to make it under different circumstances."

She took another long gulp, setting the cup down in her lap.

"What circumstances?" I urged furiously.

Her brows furrowed. "Why are you so angry?"

"You could have died!"

Eyes widening, she seemed to come to a realization. "Oh." Lifting her gaze to Fedir, she darted her eyes between us. "No. No, I wouldn't have died. I've fallen many times mid-flight and have had plenty of broken bones to prove it. If I shift at the last moment, I can slow the...the fall."

"You didn't shift," I gritted between my teeth. My head snapped back to my captain, jerking in the direction of my study.

"I'm on it," he muttered, hurrying across the room and leaving through the yellow door.

"On what?" she insisted. "What's the problem? I told you I would have made it under different circumstances." She laid her hand on my arm. I felt the cold chill of her tremble through my shirt.

"What circumstances?" I asked again, taking her hand and burying it under the warm blankets.

She scoffed. "Different ones."

"Enlighten me."

"I-I just haven't eaten well since I got here, that's all."

I bolted from the bed, flipping open her trunk. Her gowns and shoes had been placed in her wardrobe along with most of the jars she'd brought, but a few pieces of glass, blue paste, and her nuts littered the bottom. I picked one up and studied its structure between my thumb and forefinger. "You said you need these to feel normal. Why?"

She shrugged, sliding her legs slowly over the side of the bed and slipping off her shoes. "It's the only thing that seems to help how strong I feel."

Fedir returned with two books in hand. Rising from the trunk, I took one, nodding at the title.

"There's one chapter about Ravenfae history in here and this one,"—he held the thin book in front of my face—"has some information on all winged faekind. Though very little. I read it when you asked me to look into... ah—" His eyes darted to Morella, who rose on jittery legs. "When you had me looking into types of faekind before."

Morella came closer, leaning in to read the title of the book I held. "A Partial History of the Fae of Revelry?" She placed her hand on my forearm again. "This isn't a Ravenfae thing. It's a Morella thing."

"What do you mean?" I snapped the book shut, handing it to Fedir, instructing, "On my desk. Keep looking."

He nodded and left, taking both books with him.

"I mean that I've never met another Ravenfae who was as weak as I am."

My gaze darted to her hand on my arm. "You think you're

weak?"

She took her hand away and I felt the absence of it. "I know I am. I could never fly as long as the others. I could never expand my wings fully."

She demonstrated, stepping back and spanning her wings across her back. They lifted wobbly, one lower than the other as her face bunched in the effort. "See? They just didn't grow right or something."

"Has it always been this way?" I asked in a steady tone.

"Yes. Korven tried to strengthen them through exercises, but... I just never excelled at flying. It's why he's the Curse-bringer of Revelry and I am not. Even though the title should have landed with me after my mother. But Korven ensured I wouldn't have to take it. He knew I'd never be able to...to deliver curses all across the land." She shrugged in feigned acceptance. "And that's part of how I ended up here. In this marriage." Her eyes, flecked in gold, landed on mine. "With you."

I suppressed a shiver and the urge to go to her. Instead, I held out the thistle nut in my palm. "When did you discover these helped you?"

"When I was around ten."

"You don't know why they help?"

"I assume it's because of what's in them."

"And what is that?"

"I have no idea."

"You haven't researched it?"

"No."

"Why?"

She shrugged. "They've always been available to me and helped, so I haven't put much thought into them."

I tossed the blue stained nut back into her trunk. "You're not spinning today."

"Yes, I am."

"You're going to get into your bed and rest."

"I'll do just that later tonight. After you kiss me."

I swept forward so fast, she couldn't react in time. Sliding my hand behind the small of her back, I pulled her close, holding the back of her neck. I pressed my lips to hers, taking my height over her as leverage and deepening my kiss, engulfing her completely. A short "oomph" came from under my mouth somewhere, before she squeezed my arms, pulling me closer.

Over too soon, I pulled away, guiding her to her bed as she tried to regain her breath. She plopped onto the sheets and I pulled a blanket over her legs. "Get some rest. Goodnight, Moh Dhóches."

Stunned, she stared as I backed away. "But it's not even midday!" she called as I reached the study door. I didn't respond, my mind already spiraling with finding answers. The study door shut firmly behind me.

CHAPTER 19

Morella

"THA MU RE...REAMHER AGAMA." I POINTED ACROSS THE words, doing my absolute best to sound them out, which was an absolute shit job. In the common tongue, I repeated the sentence. "I have a large pig." I rolled my eyes, slamming volume one shut and tossing it on the pillow next to me.

I highly doubted Killian's true name was "pig" or "large" or any of the other simple words that littered the pages of *Céaduah, Language of the Changelingfae*. I crossed my arms and huffed like an impudent child sent to her bed early.

Too early.

I'd spent far too many hours stuck in bed with volumes of a language I was never going to learn well without actually hearing it regularly and practicing with my husband. Maybe I had a knack for it, but true understanding would never come from a dusty old book that hadn't been cracked open in a century.

Alista had come by once with a tray of fruits and cheese. I'd picked at them, stewing in the embarrassing spectacle I'd made of myself just that morning. I should have told Killian that I couldn't make it across the canyon. Instead, my Ravenfae stubbornness had wanted to try to prove I could. And now, my husband was nowhere to be found—probably scheming with Fedir on how to get rid of such a weak and damaged creature.

Tsking aloud, I sprang from my bed, landing flat on the floor a moment later with a thud. I'd seen this in myself before and knew the remedy. But the scoopful of thistle nuts I had left were in the pocket of a gown across the room in my wardrobe. Rising on wobbly legs, I made it, stuffing down a mouthful and chewing heartily, gulping them in a nut paste. They wouldn't cure me immediately, but I would be feeling stronger in the next twenty minutes or so. I slid out of my nightgown and managed to pull a clean dress from the wardrobe. When my arms got tired and my wings didn't shift right to accommodate the fabric, I tore it off in frustration, tossing the burgundy gown across the floor.

Naked, I wandered to Killian's wardrobe instead, finding pants that would never fit me and one of his soft linen shirts that draped down my legs like a dress. The front was generous in its V neckline, and in an ingenious moment, I flipped it backwards, my wings able to sit outside the shirt from the front opening. Proud of myself, I grabbed one of his neatly organized belts and wrapped it around my waist to tie off the shirt that draped to the top of my knees. A midnight blue jacket hung pressed in the back of his wardrobe, and I grabbed that, too, tying the sleeves around my waist.

Slipping on my simplest black shoes, I crept to the door, careful to open it quietly in case Killian was in his study. I stepped lightly into the corridor, shook my head at the room that he'd meant to be mine, and headed straight to the western tower to produce the day's straw into gold—just as I'd promised in our bargain.

TWO HOURS LATER, I WAS DONE, STARVING, AND struggling to keep my eyes open. I was also thoroughly put out that my husband hadn't come looking for me yet. Surely, he'd discovered I was missing? Surely, someone had?

I was used to attention. My brother was forever asking me how I was feeling or if I had eaten, or whether I'd gotten enough sleep. Even my mother watched me closely growing up, ensuring I was taking care of myself. It was a strange thing to be in a new land, in a new position, and to be left to my own wanderings.

I pressed my hand to the wheel of the spindle, taking my foot off the footman, allowing it to slow on its own and pondered my new life. Did I like having this much freedom? It was certainly... strange.

I missed some of the attention, that I could admit. But not just any attention—praise in particular. It was no wonder I'd been counting how many times my husband had complimented me. I was always seeking praise from others. My entire life, my normal was different. I couldn't keep up with the other Ravenfae children, never reaching their heights, never soaring the same skies with my friends. Compliments were few and far between, and even now, I could list each one my husband had given me.

I released the last spool of golden thread and held the bundles to my chest. Killian's jacket loosened from my waist and fell to the floor in a heap of fine silk. I folded it neatly, setting it back onto my stool, deciding it could use some embellishment at another time.

I began my shuffle down the winding staircase, muttering to myself about how I was going to find more thistle nuts when neither Killian nor Fedir seemed to know what they were.

"I distinctly remember telling you to stay in bed."

Killian's voice startled me at the end of the stairwell and I jumped, the spools of thread flying from my arms. He caught each of them with a swiftness I envied and held them in one hand.

"Well?" he asked, blocking my way through the rest of the stairwell. His gaze flitted over my attire and he frowned further. "Is that my shirt?"

I bit my cheek. The frustration coming off his body told me I might actually be in trouble this time. I decided to take an innocent approach and replied, "It was so soft and fit my wings, I couldn't help but wear it."

His eyes narrowed and I gulped, clasping my hands in front of me. "Only to the tower and back. No one saw me..."

"And that was luck," he finished.

I decided to change the subject. "How long have you been waiting here?"

"Why did you leave your bed?" he retorted.

"I made a bargain," I said simply. Pointing at the spools, I added, "Three spools of straw turned to golden thread. Though I will need a few more spools for tomorrow's quota."

"You will not be spinning tomorrow or the next day or the next until you have returned to full health." His eyes darted to my wings, which sagged on my back.

"Nonsense," I said flippantly. "I can manage—"

"I don't care what you can *manage*. You will be resting until you have your strength back. Thistle nuts will arrive tomorrow and you will be given other remedies for your...condition."

I scoffed. "My *condition*?" I stepped down two more stairs, finally meeting him in his own towering height. "I've managed my condition for longer than you've even known of my existence, husband, so your assistance is unnecessary." I scrunched my nose, adding, "Except the thistle nuts. I'll take those."

He lifted his chin, not backing down, but I didn't really expect him to. "Are all Ravenfae as stubborn as you?"

"Ha!" I laughed in his face, poking a finger in the soft part of his shoulder, finding just more solid mass instead. "And what about you?"

"I'm not stubborn. I am practical."

"Oh, yes," I mocked, "the great King of the Citrine Cliffs is so practical in his bargains, and compliments, and kisses for his wife—after all, why do more than what's strictly necessary to get your wife to give you what you need?"

"You don't know what I need. And you're obsessed with me praising and kissing you."

"Am not," I replied quickly, backing up a step to remove myself from the heat of his stare.

He followed, closing the distance between us. "Are so."

I huffed again in the most unladylike manner, leaning back but refusing to move further. "I am not."

"You are," he repeated.

His face hovered over mine and my heart beat wildly at the heat of his body so close. He carried not a wrinkle nor fine line, his face an ode to a marble carving, chiseled over years to perfection. If he was seven years older than me, he didn't look it. Faekind spent most of their lives appearing to be around thirty years old until they hit a few centuries and began to age dramatically. "How—" I swallowed hard, regaining my breath. "How old are you again?"

His lips parted slowly. "How old do you think I am, Goldling?"

"By the way you speak to me?" I snapped. "Five."

He hummed low, his fingers trailing the side of my shirt before he gripped the loose fabric in his hand. "And how old do you think I am by the way I look at you?"

My breath caught in my chest and he posed his face directly over mine, pulling on the fabric of my makeshift dress until my body was flush with his. He looked at me with nothing short of lust—of desire and want—all the things I'd felt since knowing him. I grabbed his forearms, not pushing him away but not exactly pulling him closer, either.

"Moh Dhóches," he whispered.

"Tell me what it means," I breathed.

"You will learn," he said simply, shifting his hand to rest underneath my backside. He blinked several times, almost shaking his head, adding, "And you will rest."

He lifted me and I squeaked, finding myself hauled over his shoulder, his arm wrapped around the back of my thighs. He turned with me like a sack of potatoes—a *winged* sack of potatoes—and ignored my half-hearted protest as we left the stairwell.

I'd never been carried like this before. Certainly never by my only previous lover, Brekkan Dioltry. And certainly not by my practical husband whose thumb continuously rubbed the soft skin of my inner thigh. Could he tell I loved this? Did he know that my small protest and cursing was nothing more than a show? If he only knew that I'd rather he carried me around this way often, preferably into his great big bed so he could devour me whole until I didn't know either one of our names.

As soon as the stone hall produced a wooden door, we were through it, shifting through two more until he stepped out of our own and lowered me to the floor. I clasped his forearms tightly, regaining my footing.

He jerked his head. "Bed. Now."

"Fine," I grumbled. "You don't have to be so Goddessdamn grumpy about it."

I thought I heard a chuckle but didn't turn around. The truth was, I really did need rest. I shuffled to my bed and slumped, kicking off my shoes, tossing the belt onto his bed, and pulling my sheets over my body.

"You're sleeping in my shirt?" he asked, sliding out of his jacket and hanging it back into his wardrobe.

I smoothed my cheek onto the pillow, closing my eyes and murmuring, "It's this or naked, husband."

"Go to sleep, Morella," he muttered somewhere near my bed.

"Stop talking, then."

"Córrch, Moh Dhóches."

"I'll *rest* when you stay quiet."

The bed sagged and his hand grazed my cheek. I peeked one eye open.

"What did you say?" he asked in a wide grin, staring down at me like I was a Goddessdamn blessing of a wife.

"What?" I stumbled, turning to lie on my back.

"How did you know 'córrch' means 'rest'?"

"Fucking hell, Killian." I grabbed the first volume of *Céad-uah, Language of the Changelingfae* from somewhere beneath my sheets and chucked it into his lap.

He caught it in his hands, that stupid grin there again. "You catch on quickly."

"That one doesn't count," I mumbled, my eyelids drifting. He quirked a brow and I continued through a yawn. "That compliment—you've given me that one already."

A deep rumble came from his chest and he locked me in— both of his arms on either side of me, pushing into the bed. "Am I not allowed to repeat my compliments?"

My eyes shot open in annoyance. "Of course you are, but maybe after you have a few dozen under your belt."

He leaned forward and all I could see was him. "My shirt has never looked so good as it does on you."

Even through the mounds of blankets covering my body, I shivered, suddenly very aware that I was underneath my husband. He took my chin in his hand, leaning down and whispering above my lips, "Ann córrch, banabh brèagha."

He kissed me with lips that parted only slightly and pulled away before I was anywhere near done with him. He left my side and I remained, grinning like a fool.

Rest, beautiful woman.

DAWN CAME AND I MISSED IT. LATE MORNING LED TO early afternoon, and still I slept. By mid afternoon, I stretched, burrowing my head into my pillow, my body sore from so much sleep.

"Does the exhaustion always take you to twelve hours of sleep?" My husband's voice rumbled from somewhere near my bed and I smiled, soaking in the slow rise from sleep with him nearby.

"Yes," I yawned, turning on my back and stretching my hands up to my headboard.

When I opened my eyes, I found him in a chair at my bedside, arms resting on his thighs and eyes roving over my body in his shirt. I kicked away the sheets, revealing all of the *beautiful woman* he had ordered to rest.

My shirt has never looked so good as it does on you.

A smirk drifted over my mouth and I locked my gaze with his, refusing to let go.

"*Morella*," he rasped.

I lifted myself up to sit, folding my legs underneath me. "Yes?"

He opened his mouth to speak, but held back whatever he was going to say. Instead, he took the plate on the bedside table and positioned it between us. "You need to eat this."

That black circle of meat was sliced into three thick pieces. I reared back in disgust. "No, thank you," I squeaked.

He shook his head, grabbing a fork and cutting a bite-sized piece. "Fedir believes we've identified your condition, and if he is correct, it's easily remedied."

"With this?" I asked incredulously, turning my head again when he offered the bite.

"Iron. Your blood lacks or cannot retain it. These nuts,"—he pulled a small jar of thistle nuts from his pocket—"contain a high amount of iron, which is why they help you. This, however,"—he waved the fork in front of my face again—"contains three times the amount of iron and will be a far more beneficial food for you to consume regularly."

I eyed the fuilhe with doubt. "Why does he believe this is my condition?"

"Exhaustion, dizziness, and cold hands are all symptoms. It's more common in women due to their cycles and from how you describe that you've always been somewhat...weaker than other Ravenfae, this makes the most sense."

I shrugged, my stomach churning at the evidence that added up. "Maybe I'm just cursed. And I don't have cold hands."

"Are you cursed, Morella?"

I thought briefly of my life and how everything was a struggle. Including getting my husband to do husbandly things. But there he was, sitting at the edge of my bed, offering food to help me feel stronger.

I shook my head in a solid no.

He set the fork on the plate and held his hand out between us, palm-up.

I placed my hand in his and he wrapped his fingers around mine. "Cold," he confirmed softly. "Just like every time you've touched my arm, your hands have been cold."

"Oh," I mumbled, pulling my hand back. But his fingers trapped it there as he met my gaze again.

He picked up the fork with his other hand and offered the fuilhe for the third time. "Please cooperate."

I leaned forward, opening my mouth and pulling the meat from the fork. He watched me chew slowly, tracking my movements as I swallowed.

"Good, Moh Dhóches," he praised. Instant heat coursed through me, tingling my nerves. He cut pieces for me one by one until I'd managed to consume all three circles, all while murmuring variations of how well I was doing.

Good. That's it. A little more, Moh Dhóches.

When I was finished eating and he was finished hand feeding me, he rose, stalking across the room to open the washing room door. "A bath has been drawn and everything you need for the day is here. Take your time."

I scooted to the edge of the bed, following him into the washing room to see a steaming bath, a fresh towel, and a new gown, simple and dark red.

I picked it up, clutching the soft linen to my body. "Are we going somewhere?"

"Yes," he replied with an irritating simplicity.

I rolled my eyes while turning to hide my smile. "Enlighten me," I returned, repeating his own favorite phrase.

He opened the door, ready to leave. "We're going into the town of Cenmar with Captain Fedir. To *cleadha.*"

Cleadha, cleadha, cleadha....

My mind raced, trying to pick up what the word meant.

He stared across the steam, waiting for me to catch up.

"To... to practice?" I finally suggested.

His face relaxed and he nodded. "To *cleadha*, Moh Dhóches."

CHAPTER 20

Killian

WE TOOK A SIMPLE CARRIAGE ACROSS THE GREEN FIELDS to the largest town in the Citrine Cliffs. Cenmar was the hub of trade to the other kingdoms in Revelry, which made it full of humans and faekind alike, along with different languages. Céaduah was common, especially in the sections of town where the locals purchased their goods and lived if they worked in the castle.

Hoods up and cloaks drawn, Fedir and I guided Morella through the streets, desiring to be unrecognized during our short trip. Of course, no one would know Morella. Her wings were hidden well and she had not been queen long enough to have her likeness painted or her breathtaking smile known and her laughter heard among my people.

We walked the rows of tents in the market and she listened carefully, picking up on the haggling of prices and banter between merchants and patrons of their wares.

I brought her to a stall of silks, naming each color and having her repeat after me. Fedir lingered behind us, watching the crowd and winking at a variety of beautiful faces.

Morella's fingers trailed over all the fabrics and she rubbed a few between her fingers, commenting in broken Céaduah on their texture.

Her gift for picking up the language was staggering. It had taken me years to really grasp it enough to regularly speak it, and not for the first time, I guessed that being part Changelingfae meant she had an affinity for it.

We spent the day wandering, speaking, practicing the language I needed her to know. I needed her to understand its intricacies. I needed her to know it on a level where she dreamed in Céaduah. We snacked on roasted nuts and fresh cheeses melted over toasted bread. As the sun began to lower and her feet shuffled heavily across the cobblestones, we moved on to a small tavern at the end of the market street. We ordered dinner and settled into a booth at the back, away from the crowd.

"What else would you like to see in Cenmar?" I asked as she tore into her mutton pie.

She took a long swallow of ale before answering in Céaduah. "Creags? I overheard the word a few times and assumed it's a place."

Fedir smirked, folding his arms and settling himself back into his side of the booth, waiting for my answer.

I cleared my throat and wiped my mouth. "I already tried to show you the cliffs and you fell out of the sky."

"Creags is cliffs?" she asked.

"The Citrine Cliffs," Fedir answered. "The same cliffs you need to stand on and say his true name."

She gasped and leaned forward, whispering harshly across the table. "You know about our bargain? Do you know his name? And why do I have to stand there?"

Fedir joined her in a conspiratorial murmur. "I do, no, and because that's part of his bargain with Céad."

She inhaled loudly again, turning to me sitting beside her with an enormously charming open-mouthed grin. "You made a bargain with Céad? You didn't tell me that part!" She grabbed my forearm and jostled it.

"He can't tell you anything, my queen," Fedir continued and I nodded for him to explain. "You see, when King Killian was young, he was a powerful Forestfae. He could shift through the trees just as any other, yes, but he could also...change them."

"Change them how?" she insisted, squeezing my arm.

"Our young Killian here could change the trees into sentient beings. A new kind of fae he called Dryads."

"But that's..." she glanced back at me.

"A fae Goddess trait, yes," I finished. "Keep listening."

Fedir continued, pushing his plate and mug aside. "When the Forestfae Goddess Fiola found out, she went straight to Céad who had been searching for an heir to take her place. Killian's power of such enormous change might interest her."

"And did it?"

Fedir nodded. "It angered Céad as well. The line of a Goddess's power does not often fall to men, so why would one have so much of it? And one who had no Changelingfae lineage?"

I shifted uncomfortably, rolling my shoulders. Her fingers pressed lightly to my arm and I took a deep breath.

Fedir sighed and continued. "The truth is, Queen Morella, no one knows how or why Killian had such power. But he was clever. He knew upon meeting Céad that she wouldn't think twice about ending his life and any chance of continuing this power of his on to children of his own. So he offered her a bargain. She would crown him as king of her people. He would rule all of the Citrine Cliffs and the Changelingfae and he would never create another Dryad again. He would offer his life not as her heir, but as the guiding ruler of her people, and a benevolent one at that."

Morella turned her head, giving me a dreamy grin.

"But that wasn't enough for her," Fedir continued, drawing

her attention. "He would become king, yes, but none would know his true name and Céad would take his power of change from him. He would forever be known as someone else, and if he could find someone to discover his true name, all of his power would return. Only then would he be truly known throughout the kingdom."

Morella bit her lip. "So when I figure out his name, I have to stand before the Citrine Cliffs and speak it?"

"Yes," he confirmed, catching my eye. "At dawn as the sun glints off the crystals and lines the canyon in golden light."

Morella's eyes widened as she turned to me. "Why didn't you tell me that essential detail?"

"He cannot," Fedir explained. "For part of the bargain is that he could tell only one single soul any important details on the bargain's fulfillment."

"And that's...you?"

He hummed his confirmation. "I am allowed to tell whomever I wish."

She slipped her hand from my arm, folding them in her lap with a weighted pause. A frown slowly spread across her lips and she stared at the table in front of her. Finally, she asked, "How many, Fedir?"

"Sorry?" he mumbled.

I felt the calm cold coming from her as she clarified. "How many Changelingfae have taken this bargain and tried to discover his name?"

My captain huffed a laugh, attempting to brush off the question. "I don't see how that's—"

"How many?"

I folded my arms at my chest, answering for him. "Three."

She nodded without looking my way. "And where are these Changelingfae now?" she whispered.

"Dead," I finished.

"Why?" she snapped, finally looking my way in a blaze of ire.

"My Queen," Fedir interrupted, "perhaps that's a story for another ti—"

"They entered the bargain with me," I answered.

"Killian, do you think it's wise to—"

"Ah," she started, turning her body and inching closer. "And there's the truth of it. A great king on his fourth attempt at finding someone who can discover the most basic of truths about him. This explains so much."

I bared my teeth, meeting her with my own lean into her space. "And what exactly does it explain, Goldling?"

Fedir cleared his throat. "I'll just go see about those fabrics, then."

I barely perceived his leaving.

"Your attempt at control of all things," she continued, holding my stare. "You left out that little part in our bargain. You can't change Seraphine as you are, can you?"

"No."

"You need me just as much as I need you."

"Yes." My treacherous eyes darted to her lips.

"What a fool you must think I am." She shook her head in a sneer. "Your tag-along little wife, learning the Céaduah language because maybe, *just maybe*, she'll figure out your true name and return your power. If she doesn't?" She leaned closer, fury in her eyes. "No harm done to you, right? You'll just look for another and bury her with the rest."

Her wings flared and she rose, attempting to climb over me to exit the booth. I grabbed her wrist before she could flee on golden raven wings, and we shifted through the wooden table. I held her tightly to my chest, shifting through the old wooden well bucket, next the rolling ladder of my favorite bookseller. We shifted further from town, sliding through the trees until at last I stopped.

Holding her arms at her side and pressing her back to my chest, we landed under the trees at the precipice of the Citrine

Cliffs—exactly where she was meant to fly that day I showed her the library. The wind rose, pulling hair from her braid in black wisps. I leaned down, whispering in her ear, "You will discover my true name, Moh Dhóches." I swept her hair back from her face, gathering the bundle of long, thick strands in my hand, tugging them gently so her head fell back and she could meet my eyes. "You will say it here, before the next ten weeks are over when the golden light of dawn hits this very spot."

She wiggled an arm free and wrapped her fingers over my hand at her neck. "If I'm not dead fir—"

I grabbed the base of her chin, closing her mouth before she could finish. "Oh, no, Moh Dhóches, there is no death coming to you. I'll make sure of that."

Her breath caught and her eyes of speckled gold flickered over mine with an intensity I did not expect. A longing in her gaze pierced me and sharpened my grin. I slid my fingers from her chin, trailing them slowly down her neck, exposed and soft. "Do you enjoy being held this way?" I questioned, my hands softly following the slope of her chest.

She inhaled sharply when I reached her belly, pressing so she lay flush with my own body. "Maybe I enjoy it, too." I shifted, allowing my hard cock to lay flush with her back. I chuckled softly as her eyes widened in an understanding of what she did to me.

In a flash of feathers, she turned, slipping out of my grasp and pressing her chest flush with mine. Grabbing the lapels of my jacket, she pulled herself up to murmur near my lips, "You are nothing more than talk, Killian." She slid her hands under the midnight silk, running the pads of her fingers across my skin. "You could have had me any way you like by now, but you've chosen to keep yourself at arm's length and omit some very pertinent information about what happens to the fae you bring into your bargains."

Catching her wrist, I pulled her knuckles to my lips. "You would have said no. I needed you to say yes."

She shook her head. "Our marriage contract says three months and either of us can give this up...what happens to you in three months, Killian?"

Goddess, she was clever. "I cannot tell you," I paused, lifting her chin for emphasis. "...Moh Dhóches."

She caught my hint instantly, her brows narrowed in thought. "My...something," she started. "My...chance? My...my last chance?"

I shook my head softly, still holding her hand and pressing it to my heart. "My future now lies with you. As soon as you entered that bargain, you sealed it. You control what happens on this cliff less than ten weeks from now. *You*, Morella."

A shiver racked through her body and she nodded. "Moh Dhóches," she repeated. "My Fate."

CHAPTER 21

"WHERE DO YOU THINK YOU'RE GOING?" KILLIAN demanded to know as I slipped on my shoes and wrapped myself into my dressing robe.

We'd left the cliffside across the vast valley silently, passing through trees and doors until he'd deposited us in our room. Without a word, we went about our ways, both lost in thought, both exhausted and preparing for sleep. But I had a little energy left and I needed a place to think. Spinning had always brought me comfort in the way the wheel kept time to the push of my foot and the smooth slide of wool through my fingers. I looked down at my fingers then, feeling for the small blisters forming from spinning straw instead.

"Three spools of golden thread," I explained. "I will keep all parts of my side of the bargain, husband, regardless of how tired I am."

He sprinted across the room in his large stride, grabbing hold of my arm before I could open the bedroom door. "We've been over this. You are to rest. You can take up spinning again when your body is properly fueled."

"I'm just sitting there," I retorted. "It's not like I'm roaming around a city for hours on end." I pulled myself from his grasp, but he was in front of me before I could reach the handle.

"Your Changelingfae magic drains you more than you've realized. It's why you slept so long even though you had your usual amount of thistle nuts."

Maybe he was right. I did eat the last of them that day and still I slept through it. "Well," I started, "You've fed me enough of that fuilhe. I think I can handle an hour of work."

"No, Morella, you will not spin tonight."

I clenched my teeth and glared. He was far too big for me to ever have the upper-hand on strength and by the way he planted his feet and folded his arms at his chest, I knew there was no pushing him aside in my future either. Rolling my eyes, I decided to try again later. I could stay awake and wait for him to sleep and then—

"I see you scheming, Goldling," he added with stern precision. "Let it go. It doesn't change anything in our bargain if you miss a few days." His smile was all teeth as he leaned forward. "Maybe I'll have you make up the days you miss."

I scrunched my face in annoyance, nodding slowly, pretending defeat. "Fine. You win." I pulled the tie off my robe and turned, striding across the room and tossing the creamy lace over my dressing screen. Without another word, I calmly folded back my bedding and slid between my sheets, blowing out the candle at the table between our beds and offering a simple, "Goodnight."

I nestled down, turned away from where I heard him walk across the room, approach my bed and light the match.

I bolted upright, irritated, tired, and out of patience with his little games. "What in all of fucking Revelry are you—"

He lit the candle and leaned in, his lips hovering over mine. "I have not kissed you goodnight, and I will not do so in the dark."

His head tilted and I laughed, scooting back and away, missing his kiss. "No spinning, no kiss."

"Morella," he grumbled.

My heart raced beneath my ribs. I had him. I actually finally had him. He *wanted* to kiss me goodnight. My plan had worked, it seemed, but now, I was annoyed. Men, in my short experience, were blundering fools who didn't recognize their own desires until they didn't have access to them.

I shook my head, holding back a smile and repeating his own words. "No, Killian, you will not kiss my lips tonight."

A muscle ticked in his jaw and his eyes narrowed. "You'd use my words against me?"

I lifted my chin, unable to hold back my grin of triumph in our little play of control. "I believe I just did."

A hearty laugh left his chest and he threw back my sheets, finding my legs and tugging under my knees, pulling me to the edge of the bed. He fit himself between them, lowering to the floor.

"What in the fucking hells are you doing!" I shouted, attempting to wiggle out of his hold.

Wrapping my legs around his torso, he held them to his sides. "Our bargain said I would kiss you goodnight every night. It was you who never specified where."

My eyes grew to the size of saucers as he slipped his hands under my nightgown, bunching the crimson fabric to my waist. At his touch, my skin prickled and my belly folded in on itself, tightening in a painful yearning.

He kissed the inside of my knee softly, meeting my eyes. "Now that can count as my kiss goodnight." He smoothed his hand up my thigh, slipping his fingers under the band of my silk undergarments. "But if you'd let me," he continued, trailing more kisses along my skin, "I have another place in mind."

A half moan escaped my throat as he reached the apex of my thighs, softly pressing his lips to the fabric separating him from my most tense bundle of nerves. Lowering himself further on the floor, he kept my gaze, bringing more of his mouth over me. The silk bunched against my skin and another squeak left my chest.

"Have you ever been kissed here, Moh Dhóches?"

I felt the heat of his breath at the question and I shook my head, watching in fascination as he slowly pulled the fabric from my body, exposing me to the dim light and his own eyes as he devoured me whole.

"Banabh brèagha," he whispered.

Beautiful woman.

His grip on my legs tightened as he pulled me even closer to the edge of the bed.

"I—"

He looked up at me from the floor. "Tell me if you don't want me here."

"I do!" I cried. "I just... I just don't know what I'm supposed to do."

At that, he lifted himself, wrapping his arms around my waist and meeting me face-to-face. "Are you untouched, Morella?"

"No!" I laughed nervously, adding, "I've had sex before!"

Rubbing my back softly, he asked, "How many times?"

"Twice."

"With the same person?"

I nodded, refusing to look away. "Brekkan Dioltry. We were nineteen."

"Brekkan?" He frowned. "What kind of name is Brekkan?"

"Oh, like you're one to talk," I snapped. "You have no business judging names."

"Fair enough," he chuckled. "And did you enjoy Brekkan Dioltry's company in bed?"

I swallowed hard, feeling every place he touched me like fire. "No," I whispered.

His hands inched me even closer. "And when you touch yourself, Morella, do you enjoy it then?"

I hadn't noticed how close his face had gotten to mine. He hovered over my lips. "Sometimes," I breathed between us.

He slid his fingers down my arm, taking my hand in his. "Show me where."

I took it, sliding his fingers down my chest, to my stomach, tightly coiled, until I pressed them to the most sensitive part of my body. The one place I'd explored and the only place I really knew could undo me.

He pressed his thumb to my clit, circling in slow motions and I released a soft moan from my lips.

"Is this the only place?" he asked, watching my face with a dark heat that would consume me if I didn't keep my wits.

"Yes."

He nodded, continuing his touch. "There's more to discover. But let's start here." Kissing my chest, he followed the pattern of my nightgown, settling down again on the floor between my legs. "All you need to do is tell me if you like or don't like what I'm doing. Give into your body's response and tell me to stop if you want me to stop. There are no rules other than what you decide."

Nodding, I shifted, my legs opening wide as he wrapped his arms around them, first smoothing his hands over everything exposed before him.

"I-I like that," I managed to breathe.

His eyes of brilliant blue heated beneath me as his fingers trailed over me again. "Good girl, Morella. And this?"

Spreading me open with one hand, I gasped as his mouth covered my skin. His tongue pressed gently, sending fire through my bones, spreading pleasure through my veins, and I could not imagine more bliss than this. There could not be more than this single moment when his mouth pulled away gently, softly sucking my clit between his lips. As his gaze reached mine, I felt the cruel, cold sting of air.

I wanted heat. I *needed* the warmth of his mouth.

More, more, more, until I was sick of it. Until I had to crawl away just to survive the onslaught of pleasure my husband could bring to what was slick between my thighs.

"Again," I begged, reaching out to pull him back in. "Do it again."

THE WOMAN COULD SCREAM.

And buck her hips.

And learn.

All it took was a little guidance and encouragement with my tongue and Morella had herself figured out. Within five minutes of sucking, and tasting, and licking, she'd taken me to the floor, riding my tongue and cursing in pleasure.

If I hadn't been so Goddessdamned turned on, I might have counted the number of times *fuck* came out of her gorgeous mouth, often followed by my name. As she ground herself over my face, crying out, screaming, and moaning, I withdrew my cock, fisting it with one hand and keeping her body pressed to my mouth with the other.

Her moans grew higher-pitched and I readied myself to end with her. One final slide of her over the flat of my tongue and she was there, practically collapsing on top of me as I finished in my hand, grunting in the effort it had taken to give her just this.

Only this.

"*Killian*," she breathed, collapsing onto the floor beside me.

I wasn't sure what to do. It was over and I couldn't hold her. I couldn't pull her into my bed and tuck her into my arms, kissing her hair and trailing my hands over her soft feathers.

The pleasure we'd shared began to shift into panic and I sat up quickly, tucking myself back into my pants and bolting for the door. I checked the lock, pulling on the handle and pressed my ear to the wood, listening for movement.

She couldn't do that again.

My Goldling was loud in her fucking, but if Céad had spies who thought we were—

"What is it?" she whispered next to me, pressing her own ear to the door in a frown.

"Nothing," I replied, moving away and brushing my hair back from my face. I smelled like her. And I wasn't washing it away tonight.

I pulled her from the door, guiding her back to her bed. She leapt in, sighing in the soft sheets and stretching as I pulled them over her shoulders. "Goodnight, Morella," I whispered, brushing away the hair on her cheek and blowing out the candle.

She was fast asleep in minutes.

THE NIGHTMARES BEGAN THE SAME.

Golden sun.

Blood.

Screams.

Guilt.

Years and years of guilt for the women who had been slaughtered by the insane Goddess of the Changelingfae.

By the time I recognized I was dreaming, I understood that this dream was different. Feathers tipped in gold and marred by thick red blood pooled in my bed. A form lay under the sheets that I couldn't bear to see.

It's a dream. It's only a dream.

With the force of a rope tugging at my waist, I stepped across our room, barefoot and leaving prints of blood in my wake. I stood over my bed, slowly reaching for the sheets to pull them back and witness what I'd seen thrice before.

But not like this. I'd been a young king when the women I cared for were murdered. I hadn't cared for one since, choosing instead to remain alone outside of the occasional trip to town to find quick pleasure in a woman's mouth.

The body under the sheets didn't move. A stain spread slowly across the soft white and even though I screamed in my head, telling myself to stop, still I reached down to see what I'd caused.

What I'd caused again.

"Killian!"

The shout of my name came with a slap on my cheek and my eyes flew open. The room was dark, but moonlight fed through the curtains billowing from the open window. I recognized Morella hovering over me with fear.

"You were dreaming," she urged, shaking my shoulders, slick with sweat.

I bolted from the bed, pushing her behind me, my eyes searching for signs of the body I'd just seen there.

"It was just a dream," she murmured softly, brushing her hand over my forearm.

I raced to the open windows, shutting them soundly before lighting a candle. I rubbed my face, taking a moment to breathe deep.

It was just a dream.

There was no body.

There would be no body.

I heard her light steps over our floor, bringing herself to me.

"Dè...das...ur omh a dhèana?" she whispered, pulling my hands from my face.

What can I do?

I took my hands gently from hers, replying, "Amar."

Her eyes narrowed for a moment as she thought. "Water? Wait, no...a bath!" She took my hand again excitedly, leading me to the door of our bathing chamber.

"Oh," she said as she led me to the wood tub. "There's water here already." She dipped her hand in. "But it's gone cold. Let me see if I can get—"

"No." I grabbed her arm. "The dreams come often. The cold water helps clear my head."

I set the candle on the basin sink and let my cotton pants slide to the floor, not caring if she saw me naked. She watched in silence as I slid into the cold water, instantly relaxing and coming back to the space I knew.

In the dim light, I breathed deeply.

It was only a dream.

It was only a dream.

"Do you need anything?" she whispered somewhere behind me.

"No. Thank you. Please go back to bed, Morella."

Her hand brushed across my head in a soothing gesture and she left, closing the door softly behind her.

I waited in the silence, searching for the calm reassurance of my steady heartbeat.

It did not come.

Morella was there, a doorway away, and as much as I wanted to relax, something prickled in my mind. She had agreed to stay in our room instead of spinning, and she'd done it with little argument, which wasn't like what I knew of her at all.

With cold water splashing over the sides of the tub, I threw myself out, barely wrapping a towel around my waist before I tossed open the door connecting the rooms. "Morella!" I called, throwing back her sheets to find her bed empty.

"Killian?"

I darted to the other side of her dressing screen, finding her there holding a bundle of sheets in her arms. "What is it?" she asked, tossing the sheets on her trunk and gripping my shoulders.

I hung my head, taking more deep breaths. I wouldn't be sleeping tonight, that I knew. "Nothing," I said, pulling a hand through my hair. "It's nothing. Please get some more rest. I won't bother you again."

I headed to my drawers for fresh clothes, searching for something lightweight to wear by the fire I'd build for the rest of the night. I couldn't go to my study as I typically would. My fear wouldn't let me leave this room until daybreak and Morella rose in a few more hours—of that, I was sure.

She headed back towards her bed, calling, "It's no bother, Killian, truly. I can't imagine having recurring nightmares. I hardly remember my dreams at all."

"You are Goddessblessed then, to sleep so peacefully." I dressed in loose cotton pants and shirt and bent at the fireplace, adding the kindling. Checking on her again, I found her fluffing the pillows on my bed and rolling back the sheets, slapping at them until they lay flat and pristine. "What are you doing?"

"Changing your sheets, of course. They were rather damp and fresh bedding is one of the best comforts in all of Revelry, if you haven't noticed." She threw a softer woven throw up into the air, taking care to pull it up just so—swiping her hands across the soft threads.

"Thank you," I said, lighting the fire. "But I won't be sleeping the rest of the night. Please go back to bed. Dawn is only a few hours away."

I sighed deeply, falling back into my chair and picking up one of the books on faekind Fedir had left me. Seconds later, I heard her own long sigh as she settled into the chair across from mine, hair tied back on top of her head and legs folded up into her seat.

I watched in rapt fascination of this creature who had flipped my life upside down in the past three weeks as she settled herself with the blue woven throw wrapped over her lap. Without so much as a glance in my direction, she opened volume two of *Céaduah, Language of the Changelingfae*, and began to read in silence.

"Morella," I called, in a trying tone.

"Hmm?" she answered, keeping her eyes on the book over her lap.

"I told you to go back to sleep."

She shrugged in indifference, still not looking up. "So you did."

"You needn't stay up on my account. I'm fine."

"Didn't say you weren't," she replied flatly.

Vexing woman.

A low grumble left my chest. I decided on another tactic. "If this is a ploy to stay up until I doze in my chair so you can sneak off to spin straw, it won't work. I won't be falling asleep and have excellent hearing."

She snorted at that, her eyes finally lifting from her book to glance behind me. I turned in my seat, following her gaze, squinting at three spools of golden thread stacked on the small writing desk by the door.

"*Morella,*" I scolded.

"We're even tonight, husband. We've both kept to our bargain."

Goddess, her face. Her black hair bundled in a frizzy bun atop her head. The soft brown of her eyes with shimmers of gold and the narrow slant of her nose. Her high rounded cheeks and beautiful lips flushed with delicate red.

I remained silent, keeping her stare, her challenge, and her crumbling hold on what I couldn't afford to give her.

Her lips parted slowly and she swallowed, gently closing her book. "I'm curious..."

"Yes?" I replied instantly.

"The way you kissed me tonight..."

The way I'd kissed her.

Flashes of her body perched over my mouth ran through my thoughts.

"You regret it?" I asked tentatively, setting my elbow on the arm rest and my chin on my fist.

She shook her head quickly, unfolding her legs beneath her. "No, that's not it at all! I'm just curious if—if I could do to you what you...I mean not the exact same, of course, but could I also...kiss you like that?"

I stared in stunned silence. "You wish to?"

She rose from her chair, folding the blanket into pristine, even squares. "If I did..."—her eyes rose to mine—"would you teach me?"

I cleared my throat, doing what I could to remain calm. "Brekkan Dioltry did not teach you?"

She shook her head, stepping closer. "I did not wish to ask."

I snapped my jaw tightly, my nostrils flaring as she continued to move forward, closing the gap between us. Her neatly folded blanket flopped to the floor and she followed on her knees before I could react. She leaned in, settling her chest between my legs, keeping my gaze as she slid her hands down my cotton pants.

"You wish me to teach you, Goldling?"

Her fingers brushed closer. "I've wished for you to teach me many things, husband. I see now I need to be more direct with what I want from you, and right now, I want you to teach me about this..."

Her hand lay flat against my cock, stiff and throbbing, though I kept the rest of me taut. I inhaled in a deep shudder, my breath releasing in a low grumble through my chest as her thumb stroked the underside of my dick.

Goddess, she had the power to destroy me and she didn't have any clue. The night was dark and we'd already explored the attraction between us, so what was a little more in the lessons of pleasure?

I shook my addled head, still deciding, running a hand over my mouth when she leaned further still. "I'm a quick learner, if that is your hesitation. It will not take long for you to teach me this skill."

"You believe my hesitation is that you will be bad at this?" I laughed low. "Morella, you could merely breathe in my direction and I would use such a sweet sound to please myself for decades to come."

Her eyes widened and mouth parted again. *Shit.*

I adjusted myself slightly in the seat, forcing my hands to stay on the armrest where they needed to stay.

Another of her smiles bloomed across her mouth. "I'll take that as a compliment number six. What is your hesitation, then, husband?"

"That I'll want more," I whispered honestly.

She took her own moment to think before shaking her head, her bun of hair waving in the movement. "This is just a kiss. Just my kiss, Killian. That's all it needs to be, if you'd like."

Making my decision, I tapped my lips. "You start here, Moh Dhóches. Your kiss tonight starts here."

CHAPTER 23

Morella

I ROSE TO MEET HIS LIPS, SOFT AND QUESTIONING. HE feared he'd want more. But I wanted him to want more. To share our bodies in pleasure would be a gift and I felt like we were close. So close to something I could taste, and feel, and see for our future.

I deepened the kiss, playing with his tongue as a promise of what I could do. His hands stayed gripped to the chair, but mine did not. They were everywhere on his skin—his neck, his arms, his chest. Goddess fucking dammit, his *chest*. I did what came naturally. I unbuttoned his nightshirt, opening the front so I could move my mouth across his skin—something I could never tire of.

He was so large in that chair by that fire in that room, and I wanted to lick everything—everywhere—until my tongue had consumed every surface of his skin and he was left moaning *my* name. I only desired to undo his mind like he had mine, and I would do so by the tongue I had trailing across the plain of muscle just above the hem of his pants. My hands continued their wandering, now digging into the skin at his hips.

I slowed my trek down his body, looking up to meet his stare.

I'd never been looked at in such a way.

The heat radiating from his gaze had me grinning in triumph as my kiss sank lower, lower, and lower still until I could not avoid the hard length of him still tucked behind the soft cotton.

"Where do I kiss next?" I asked.

"Something tells me you know," he growled.

I nodded, pulling myself away from his delectable torso, peeling back the hem of his pants in rapt fascination.

I'd never seen one this close before and something twisted uncomfortably low in my belly like a part of me was waking— demanding and wild.

"Here?" I asked sweetly, pressing a soft kiss to the head of his cock. His cum glistened already and more excitement pooled through me.

From the corner of my eye I saw his hands grip the chair tighter, bringing out the white of his knuckles.

"Good, Morella," he whispered low. "Take my cock into your hand and slide it up and down. Kiss where you think you should. Watch my body for signs of what I enjoy most from your mouth."

I gripped the length of him in my hand, relishing in the soft warmth. It was harder than I thought and with the first stroke, more spilled from the tip.

"Is this a sign?" I asked, before sweeping the length of my tongue across the head of his cock to taste him.

"*Morella*," he growled, his throat rough, his hands betraying him completely, while his fingers dug into the armrests of the chair as if he'd soon tear them off.

I remembered the heat of his mouth on my most sensitive nerves and how much I hated when he'd move away, so I licked again, this time pausing a moment before lowering my mouth over him, not quite all the way, but enough to taste more of him, and give him my own warmth.

I licked him sweetly, slowly exploring more with my tongue

as I took more of him. Did he want all of me over him? I pulled him out of my mouth, stroking where my spit dripped down the full length, and looked to him for more signs.

He'd gone feral.

The flame in his gaze was wild, his eyes dilated, his chest heaving, nostrils flaring and teeth biting down so hard, his jaw kept flexing in the low firelight.

Did I have so much power over his pleasure? How could such a disciplined man lose his tightly leashed control over the mere touch and kiss of a woman?

I watched him in fascination, stroking long and slow. I'd done this to him. I'd made him look this way. Me, his wife of an arranged marriage of whom he did not even dance with on our wedding night. Of whom he tried to force into an entirely different room to sleep.

The thought made me want to laugh. What a fool my husband had been, trying to deny the instant attraction between us. Well, I wouldn't have it. I wouldn't let him do it any longer. This fire in his eyes was mine and I'd see it as often as I could.

I continued to stroke him, keeping his gaze. "Are you not glad, husband, that I pulled my trunk into this room all those nights ago?" I licked up his rigid shaft again, leaving more spit to moisten my hold as I stroked faster and he shifted forward. "Are you not pleased that I refused to be parted from you, my husband, *my* fate?" My thumb grazed over the head of his cock, catching more of his cum. "Are you not happy with the wife you bound yourself to, kissing you in such a way?"

He let go at that, one hand cupped at the base of my neck, the other sliding through my hair. "It's only polite I let you touch yourself as you finish me off, my Sweet Goldling. You must be dripping by now."

I was. Goddessdammit, I was.

I bunched my nightgown at my waist, tying the loose fabric

in a knot and slid my fingers over my skin, slick with wanton longing.

"Good girl," he whispered. His hand behind my head pulled gently on my hair and somehow, I wanted him to pull it more. "Now," he continued as my body responded to his voice, "You're going to take all of me into your mouth. I'll guide your head. Let me lead and don't come back up until my cum hits your throat."

I moaned in a short gasp as he pulled my head back further, leaning down to consume me with one of his kisses that left me utterly breathless. "You will finish with me. Are you ready?"

I nodded eagerly, diving back onto his cock with new fervor, licking, tasting, moaning as his hand pushed and pulled my mouth up and down all of his shaft. His cock hit the back of my throat as he filled my mouth completely and I sputtered for a moment.

"Take it all," he growled. "All of it, Moh Dhóches."

I regained my breath through my nose, furiously circling my clit and pressing my body against his legs, begging for him to let us both finish.

"Just like that," he grunted, now bucking his hips in time with my head. "You're doing so well, Morella. My beautiful Goldling with such a talented mouth."

His hand squeezed my hair in one tight grip and I knew he was close. "Morella," he gritted and I did little but take all of his cock and whimper as my own release neared. I just needed the full taste of him and it would be over for us both.

In a carnal groan that came from deep in his chest, he came, spilling into my mouth and I let myself go as I took it all, stubbornly refusing to spill a single drop. My own release tore through me, sending me pulsating on my knees and dripping down my own leg as I released him, gasping for fresh air.

His chest heaved as he looked down at me with eyes of brilliant blue, blazing with something I couldn't name but had seen before.

His hands stayed, but gentle as his fingers brushed my face and he wiped what was left from my bottom lip before pushing it into my mouth. My tongue came out to meet him and lapped him clean, pulling his thumb between my lips, refusing to look away.

"I want to keep you," he whispered, searching my face for... something.

I cupped my hands over his. "You have to keep me. I'm your wife."

He gulped, a shudder running through his body. "In less than three months—"

"I'll still be your wife," I finished, ready to beg for it to be true.

"Moh Dhóches," he began.

"No, Killian. It will not be me who breaks this contract." I lifted a hand to cup his cheek where he closed his eyes, leaning into my touch. "It will not be me."

A WEEK WENT BY, THEN TWO.

Each day blended into the next.

I woke each morning, put myself together with Alista's help, and met Killian in his study. He would already be working away at facts and figures, research, and projects for our kingdom.

I'd greet him warmly and kiss the top of his head, bent in concentration, where he'd grunt an acknowledgement, stubbornly refusing me any more than that.

And each morning a side cart by his desk would be laden with my breakfast: berries, nuts, tea, and of course, my daily helping of fuilhe. I would pull up a chair in front of his desk and read one of the volumes of *Céaduah, Language of the Changelingfae*, often pushing aside his work if only to catch his eye and smile as he grumbled his irritation.

When breakfast was finished and I had no real reason to stay in his study any longer other than to ponder when he was going to just give in to me, I'd head for the western tower and spin. Sometimes I'd spin for hours and hours on end, singing songs, tidying up the room, sweeping the floor, and doubling the day's quota of golden thread.

Regardless of how long I'd take, he was there at the end of the staircase each time, and I wondered if he waited all morning or periodically shifted through wooden doors to check on my progress.

I'd greet him warmly again and hand him the spools of thread, asking about his morning, to which he'd reply with the shortest possible answers. We'd eat lunch together while Fedir joined us, discussing castle business. I always listened carefully, consumed by the workings of our realm and straining to hear any hints at what could be Killian's true name.

Afterward, Fedir and I would leave, heading to the grassy fields so I could practice adjusting my wings, spreading them wide over and over to strengthen my muscles. The captain kept a notebook, jotting down all the timings of how long and far I could shift and fly as the iron in my blood kept me growing stronger each day.

By the end of the fifth week of my time as Queen of the Citrine Cliffs, I was writing another letter to Korven and Seraphine.

My dearest loves,
I cannot express my joy upon receiving your

last letter. I'm afraid Avici is blossoming and I am not there to witness. In the new year, we will visit and I will squeeze my darling girl again. The fields here are beautiful as autumn descends, and the rain is keeping everything green and lovely.

"PREPARE YOUR LIST OF NAMES TONIGHT." MY HUSBAND'S voice startled me and I turned from the small writing desk to watch him finish his shift through our bedroom door.

"Killian!" I shouted, pressing a hand to my chest. "Don't do that!"

He strode to the desk, crouching to meet my face. "The names, Morella. Have you started a list of potential names?"

"Of course I have, but—"

"Tomorrow," he interrupted. "At dawn. We go to the cliff at dawn and you will speak each one across the valley."

His face was hard—a mask I'd come to recognize. I brushed his cheek. "Did something happen?"

"No." He rose, backing away from my touch. "Our time is dwindling and we must begin your attempts."

I nodded, adopting his serious tone and quickly signed the letter, folding and stamping it with the wax seal of the Citrine Cliffs, to be delivered in the morning.

I withdrew the scroll of parchment I'd been using to jot down potential names while studying and unrolled it. "Would you like to see what I have so far?"

"No," he replied instantly, hanging up his midnight blue jacket and unbuttoning his shirt underneath.

I crossed my legs as his bare chest was revealed and stared unabashedly at his muscled torso. What did he do to keep so fit? How had muscles like that been so sculpted, so defined?

It had been almost three weeks since he'd voluntarily touched me more than our kiss goodnight. Even with those, he didn't touch more than necessary, though he took his time. Each kiss came slow and thoughtful. Each brush of our lips sending us into the quiet night as if it was all he was willing to allow.

He broke my thoughts as he returned to my side, leaning down near my lips. "I'll kiss you goodnight, Morella."

He placed his mouth softly on mine, not lingering this time, but inhaling a full breath before he turned away.

I bolted upward from my chair as he left. "Wait! Where are you going?"

He didn't turn as he continued toward the bathing chamber door. "I'm taking my bath now. You should rest early. I'll wake you an hour before dawn."

The door closed behind him and I stood alone in our room, the fire crackling, the beds turned down, my lips still blooming in the ghost of his kiss.

Three weeks.

Three fucking weeks, and I considered if I could stand many more. My body begged for more of what we had shared that night, and when I was in his presence, it was so much worse. I'd change each evening to find myself aching for his hands, my belly absolutely churning in discomfort with thoughts of everything we could have had by now.

It wasn't that he didn't want me.

Oh, no. I saw it there each morning as he stole glances while I read. It was there each day he met me in the stairwell, and there on his face as he watched me leave his side with Fedir, his eyes hard and jealous—so blatantly obvious that Fedir often turned to give him a sheepish grin to apologize for something that was Killian's own damn fault.

A lack of desire was not stopping him.

Before I'd thought through my decision, I was at the bathing room door, knocking softly. His questioning reply was muffled and I lied through my teeth. "I just forgot to tell you something. May I come in?"

Another grumbled reply didn't fool me in the slightest, and I opened the door softly, meeting a candle-lit chamber, fresh with steam fogging every surface.

His enormous frame draped over the entirety of the tub with his head leaning back against a towel, his eyes closed in the silence. "What is it you've forgotten to tell me?"

I studied the way his arms lay still, though his hands pressed tightly to the side of the tub, the raised veins striking. "I...I shifted and flew for nearly an hour today without tiring. And Fedir thinks I'll reach two hours within the month."

"Morella," he started, "you know I receive this information each day, so it is not that you have forgotten to tell me." His eyes flashed open and he caught me staring. "What is it you really wish to say?"

He had me there.

"I've just been thinking..."

He grunted in acknowledgement.

"About what you said that night you kissed me."

"I've kissed you many nights."

"The night you kissed me elsewhere."

Silence filled the room and the space between us. Finally, he closed his eyes again, replying with a short, "What of it, Goldling?"

I was not so easily fooled by his calm indifference. I knew I was there, under his skin, and he'd all but admitted it before I learned to bestow my own kiss that night upon *him*.

I stepped closer, my bare feet padding softly across the wood floor. On bended knees, I lowered myself to the edge of the tub, placing my hand on his arm, waiting for him to open his eyes and see from my face what I was telling him.

Slowly, he lifted his gaze to meet mine and I continued. "You said that night that there was more pleasure to discover." I slid my fingers down his arm, folding my hand in his. "I am here to learn."

He squeezed my fingers. "And if I no longer wish to teach you?"

I shook my head in a grin. "Do you think I do not see it?"

His jaw tightened and he took his hand away.

I continued anyway, pulling at the tie around my waist. "Do you think you hide your desire from me, husband?" I slid the soft silk off my shoulders, revealing the same crimson nightgown draped across my body. "Do you believe your feigned indifference fools me?" I traced the side of his face. "It's these eyes, Killian. I see the fire in them when you look at me. When you watch me. When you dream of tasting me again. When you touch yourself imagining my lips replacing your hand."

He caught my fingers, staring hard, that fire lighting once again. He searched my face and I refused to falter—ensuring he saw exactly what I needed him to see. "Get in," he finally grumbled.

I moved swiftly, eager to prove I was right and this wasn't all in my head. I slipped out of my nightgown and stepped into the water, lowering myself slowly in the piercing heat. The tub was enormous but between his frame and my wings, little room was left to spare.

"Turn around," he ordered. "Put your back to me. Right here," he patted his chest and Goddessdamn me, I wanted to press myself to it.

But I did as he said, relaxing my shoulders before his hands grabbed my waist and he slid me closer, pressing me against his hard length and settling me between his legs. "Lean back."

I adjusted my wings, folding them around my arms to lay flush against his chest. His hands lifted to my shoulders, pushing into my stiff muscles and driving a moan from my lips at the sweet release of tension.

"Let's begin, Moh Dhóches." His hands drew lower across my

chest, over my peaked nipples and down my belly. "Did you find release when you lay with Brekkan Dioltry?"

"It was almost ten years ago," I began, then inhaled sharply as his fingers reached my inner thighs.

"I didn't ask how long ago. I asked if his cock made you cum."

I bit the inside of my lip before answering. "No."

"And since then, have you found pleasure here?" A finger dipped inside of me, slowly and smoothly.

"Not...not really." It was true, even then with my gorgeous husband's cock pressing into my back and hand smoothing over my clit, I felt no change in pleasure with his finger inside me.

"I'd like to try something, Morella, if you trust me."

He withdrew his finger, returning to circle around my clit.

"I trust you," I whispered.

"If you find it uncomfortable—"

"I'll tell you to stop," I finished. "I understand."

"It is a shame," he continued, sliding his finger inside me again, "that you did not experience a more talented first lover, Goldling. I shudder to think of the pleasure you've missed."

His finger curved, tapping inside of me and I jerked, a thin thread of something new shifting through my body. "What—" I shifted slightly, leaning back further and pulling my legs closer to my chest. "How did you...?"

Instead of an answer, he slid another finger inside, curving them, tapping that same spot. Again, a surge of something I'd never felt raced through me and I gasped.

"There it is," he whispered, sliding his other hand across the peak of my breasts.

"There *what* is?" I asked, squirming, adjusting, my body needing to feel that again.

"That place our dear Brekkan never found."

I laughed. "You bring him up so often—is that jealousy I hear?"

His fingers began to pulse, *tap, tap, tapping* and I moaned, gripping the side of the tub, pulling one leg up further to my chest.

"Yes," he admitted as his hand left my breasts, instead cupping under my chin and forcing my head back where he covered my mouth with his own.

Tap, tap, tap—his fingers were relentless, having found the one place inside of me I didn't even know existed. It was like being woken after a thousand years to something I was meant to know—to experience, to beg for and I did. Of course I did, sweeping my lips from his if only to call his name as my body tensed, and I was flushed with bright fire in my veins, ignited from his touch.

"*Killian,*" I moaned, my breath heavy, "I don't know—what do I—"

His fingers were a torment, pressing over and over and over inside me, cupping all of me without hesitation, without a moment to process where he was bringing my body—to a place I'd never been and didn't know how to be.

"Don't hold back," he gritted, picking up his pace in response to how my body stretched, my legs now spread so wide they ached. "You're going to let me take you through all of this to the end. Look at you." His hand lifted my chin again, forcing my head back against his chest. "You're taking my fingers so well, Moh Dhóches."

Faster now, I squirmed and moaned and cried out, my body pulsing in his rhythmic tapping, stronger, harder—and I felt my body tighten, my hand digging into his arm as a final cry escaped my throat.

Before it fully left my lungs, his hand was over my mouth, muffling the sound as my body pulsed, rocking to the rhythm of his fingers still there, slowing and bringing me back down from where he'd taken me. As I whimpered, he withdrew his hand, wrapping an arm around my belly.

My legs shook, my mind swirled—lightheaded and blurry. I blinked over and over, confused and trembling. He turned me in his arms and I tried to focus on his face.

"Morella," he whispered, taking my head in his hands. "Morella, are you hurt?"

I shook my head, suddenly overcome with emotion.

I didn't cry often, but felt the overwhelming urge to do so now, even if I couldn't understand why. My chin trembled and my eyes swelled with tears.

"Moh Dhóches..." He wiped the first tear as it fell down my cheek. I swallowed hard, heavy with the realization that I'd never known this pleasure, and now, I'd only known it with him.

He kissed my forehead, laying my head on his chest as I shivered, my legs shaking with residual pulsating pleasure.

"I didn't know." I sniffed, wiping my nose. "I didn't know it could...it could be like that."

"Did...did you enjoy—"

"Yes!" I trembled, lifting my head. "It was...different from what I've explored before. You must think I'm so naive."

He stroked the top of my head. "Naivety is not always such a terrible thing. In this case, there is nothing wrong with it. You didn't know and asked me to show you. Now you know and can...experiment yourself."

"Oh, I plan to," I laughed, feeling his chuckle rumble underneath me still draped across his chest.

"We should get some rest." Wrapping his arm around my back, he rose, folding a towel around my body as he helped me from the bath. He followed next patting himself dry, still hard as ever.

"Do you want me to—" I started.

Picking up on my implication, he frowned. "Rest, Morella. We both need rest."

I nodded, lifting my nightgown from the floor and stepping

into the soft silk. He followed me out the door, donning his same white linen pants that left nothing to my imagination.

I climbed into bed, utterly exhausted, sated, and dreamy, knowing I'd drift as soon as my eyes closed on my pillow.

"Goodnight," he whispered, landing a kiss on my forehead.

Emboldened by how softly he'd held me, I reached out for his forearm, rising to my knees. "Stay?" I whispered back.

"Morella," he began, placing his hand over mine, "this is your bed and that is—"

"I know," I interrupted. "I know this is my bed and that is yours, but just...just until I fall asleep, will you stay with me?" I shifted my hand to his. "Please, Killian?"

His eyes roamed over my bed of tousled sheets and an array of pillows. He reached down, pulling a small, golden-tipped feather from the sea of white. He twisted the shaft for a moment between his fingers before deciding. "Alright. Just this once."

I bit my lower lip in excitement and triumph as he gently lay my fallen feather on the side table. I hurried to the other side of my bed, pushing away the sheets and holding them up to finally welcome my husband next to me.

He slipped inside and I curled up instantly, the ease of his warmth and familiar scent of fresh grass flooding my senses in a serene relaxation I'd never known. I buried my head into his shoulder and neck, placing a simple kiss there before sighing and closing my eyes.

My mind began to fall, but I held on so tightly, just as he held onto me, his breathing steady and deep. I wondered when he'd leave. I wondered when he'd decide that was enough of me and return to his own bed to sleep alone—where he'd slept alone all the nights of our marriage.

I didn't want him to go, nor did I want to fall asleep knowing that when I woke, he'd be gone again, and back to his usual coldness to every part of me I'd been offering him since our wedding vows.

Before too long, I couldn't hold on. I couldn't stay awake with him as hard as I tried.

His voice came soft in my hair, muffled as I drifted away to a place of deep rest. "Moh Dhóches," he whispered in the dark. "... Moh Geràdah."

My fate...My love.

CHAPTER 24

Killian

THE NIGHTMARE DIDN'T COME. THE BODY, THE BLOODY
sheets, the terror of knowing what I'd uncover and that laugh of
madness never came as I drifted unintentionally with Morella
tucked into my arms.

As clarity settled in, my eyes flew open and I found myself in
her bed, the dark still heavy, Morella still tangled up in my limbs.
Irrational fear overcame me and I bolted from the bed, throwing
back the sheets over her body, shaking her awake.

"Morella!"

She turned in half-sleep as I inspected her, searching for
blood, wounds, anything indicating Céad had come calling.

"What is it?" she asked blearily, stretching her arms over her
head.

I turned her and ignored her gasp as I inspected her wings.
Was I still dreaming? Was this some new torture to find her
asleep in my arms only to turn her over and find—

"Killian!" she called, lifting her head in irritation. "What the
fuck are you doing?"

"No wounds," I managed to say, sliding my hands down her
back, her hips, her legs—even lifting her foot to confirm she was
unharmed.

She wrangled herself free of my gasp. "Of course not! Why would you think I'd be wounded?"

I pressed my palms to my eyes, regaining my breath in heavy inhales. My mind whirled with images I'd seen over and over again in my nightmares, repeating what I'd seen in the flesh a decade ago.

She was there, wrapping her arms around me, pressing my head to her chest. "I'm alright, Killian." Her hands smoothed over my back. "I'm alright."

I took one final breath, slowly pulling out of her grasp. I met her eyes in the dark. "I fell asleep. In your bed," I mumbled.

I took several more breaths, letting myself be held before I calmly rose, reaching the edge of my bed and shaking out the neatly tucked sheets. "It won't happen again," I finished.

"But—" she began.

I turned instantly. "No, Morella. It *can't* happen again. We cannot sleep together."

Confusion and hurt crossed her face as she sank back down into her bedding. I sighed, putting on a small smile for her. "It's time to get up anyway. Dawn approaches and you have some names to call into the morning sun."

"ÓR."

Gold.

"Righór."

Golden King.

"Currag."

My head snapped up. "Carrot, Goldling?"

Morella lowered the list of names she'd been calling out into the chilled morning light, reaching up to fluff my hair as I walked past in my pacing. "I thought it was worth a try. Your hair is rather...carroty."

"Keep going," I growled, ignoring that spark in my chest at her laughter. She turned back to the cliffside edge, and I timed the light as the rays of dawn crept closer to where I stood.

"Farigh."

Fae king.

"Badia fireann."

Male goddess. I cringed at that one, hoping beyond hope that Céad was not spying on us right then.

"Righchdail."

Handsome king.

My lips tilted upwards, but I kept my pace, drawing grooves in the soil as the line of the sun crept ever closer.

"Órleanab."

Golden child.

"Coileanab."

Forest child.

"Righdàna."

Fated king. I rose a brow at that one, impressed with her use of combining words.

She listed off another twenty combinations before the sun hit my line in the dirt, signaling that the day's attempts were over.

Lowering her list and shuffling to me, she sighed. "I have more. For tomorrow, I mean."

"I didn't expect you to guess correctly the first time you tried."

She turned back to the rising sun. The rays of light sparkled off the rocky citrine, blanketing the valley below in a brilliant glow of gold.

"You'll figure it out, Goldling," I murmured, keeping my distance.

"I know," she sighed, facing me again and rolling up her parchment. "I know. I know I will, Killian. I promise."

I nodded, offering her my hand. We shifted into the dawn with less than seven weeks left for her to keep that promise.

CHAPTER 25
Morella

FEDIR UNFOLDED HIS MEASURING TOOL AND STEPPED behind me on the grassy hill. I squeezed my eyes shut and used all the muscle I had recently gained in my shoulders to span my wings as far as I could.

He made a grunt of approval and wrote a quick note in his booklet with a piece of chalk. "Your wingspan has widened by over a third since we began to increase your iron. Your growing strength is impressive, my queen."

Nodding, I shifted, soaring high above the hills to ride along the chilled wind. I flexed my muscles and soared while the captain settled into the grass to sketch and wait for me to tire. He'd been timing me for weeks now and each day, I grew stronger—able to keep my wings adrift a little longer.

It had been another week since Killian woke me in a panic. Another week of the same, except now, he woke me early each morning before dawn to declare my guesses at his name into the morning light. My husband had returned to his broody, withdrawn pretense of treating our marriage as if it were no more than a business transaction.

I, of course, understood it to be otherwise.

I circled the hill a few times before shifting out of my golden raven form and landed on the grass beside Fedir.

"Surely, you can do longer than that, Your Majesty," he mumbled, continuing his sketch of a raven along the tree line.

"I don't want to fly, Fedir. I want to talk." I sat, tucking my legs underneath my dress. "About Killian."

"I see," he said, snapping his book closed. "What is it you'd like to know about our dear king?"

"You're a Changlingfae..." I began.

"Yes, and?"

"So you have a special ability, I've heard. To *predict* change..."

"That is my Changelingfae power, correct."

"And...for Killian? Can you see the change in his future? Where his power returns because I have found his true name and his bargain with Céad has been fulfilled?"

He stared pensively at the grassy fields. "My power of foresight is not quite so detailed, Queen Morella. I do see change in his future, but..." He pulled up a blade of grass and leaned back on his elbows, chewing the sweet root.

"But?" I urged.

"But...his change involves you."

"So I do discover his name?"

"I didn't say his change is about his name."

"Well fucking Goddess take me then, Fedir," I growled in frustration. "What else could the change be?"

He raised a brow in my direction, a blooming grin on his mouth.

I heaved a sigh, pulling at the grass myself. "Your prediction is wrong there, I'm afraid. Our dear king is quite the talented liar and refuses to acknowledge our marriage in that way."

"King Killian is a fool, yes, we know that, but regardless, I've foreseen the change and you are deeply woven into it."

"Can you see exactly what it is?"

"I cannot."

"Then how can you really know that the change in our relationship is the true outcome of your prediction?"

He shrugged, lying flat on his back and folding his arms behind his head as the first drops of rain fell. "How do you know the straw between your fingers will transform into golden thread? You can feel its change right before it happens, can you not?"

I fell back, mimicking his position. "Yes, it does feel like that."

We fell silent for a moment as droplets hit our faces. "You're a good friend, Fedir." I turned and smiled. "To both of us, but especially Killian. I know it hasn't been easy for him since... whatever happened that gave him those nightmares."

His eyes darted to me briefly. "Yes. Killian has...experienced more pain than he ever deserved. I'm glad to have been his friend through all of it."

"He hasn't explained what his dreams are about," I said, catching his eye.

He sighed, rubbing his face of droplets. "He should, my queen. And he will. Give him a little more time."

I pulled at the grass, dismantling his words. The wind picked up, along with the rain. "Do you think I'll do it?" I asked softly, afraid of his answer.

"Discover his true name?" He cleared his throat, nodding his head toward the line of trees below us. Killian appeared, his bulky frame crossing the distance in long strides, his midnight blue jacket fluttering open at the chest.

I rose instantly, surprised to see him.

Fedir stood slowly, stretching and popping his back. "Yes," he said simply, taking a short knife from his belt and throwing it across the field at Killian.

I gasped in a gargled inhale as the knife shot through the rain where it clanged into Killian's unsheathed dagger, falling to the grass.

He was near enough that I heard his grumble and I pushed Fedir. "What the fuck was that for!"

"Your Majesty!" he laughed, stumbling slightly. "I'm the captain of his guard—it's my job to keep our king on his toes."

Killian approached, glaring at Fedir and sliding his dagger back into his scabbard. He held a hand out to me. "Come. We must return to the castle immediately."

I took it as he turned and pulled me along, back to the line of trees. "Why?" I asked, racing to keep up.

"Because he won't stop shouting and making unreasonable demands to see you."

"What? Who?"

He wrapped an arm around my waist, pulling me closer, easing me into his chest where my body responded instantly. Fedir grabbed his shoulder, ready to shift with us.

Killian's eyes darkened as he answered. "Your Cursebringer brother."

THE CURSEBRINGER OF REVELRY WAS IN *MY* CASTLE, shouting at *my* people, and shedding his Goddessdamn feathers all over *my* foyer.

Despite my own personal diplomatic treatment of the arrival of the brother to the queen, Prince Korven managed to insult my entire kingdom as he demanded to see his sister immediately, threatening to 'tear this castle down brick by fucking brick' until she was produced.

But now, Korven and Morella argued in barely-contained whispers at the copper fountain in the grand foyer, both of their sets of wings flaring with equal intensity.

"Do you know what this is about?" Fedir whispered to me as we leaned against the far wall, giving the siblings space. I wasn't going to give them privacy, though. Not when the Cursebringer was flailing his arms about so wildly with a range of fear in his eyes.

I shook my head at Fedir's question, refusing to look away as Korven caught my glare before going back to arguing with his sister.

"It was a mistake!" she finally shouted, changing her harsh

whisper into an echoing confession instead. She pointed back to me. "He has been helping me, Korven! I just forgot to add—"

Her brother cut her off, storming closer to me, pointing his finger as well. "He could be threatening you even now, Morella. You *said*. You *promised* every letter you sent would include it and it's not like you to simply forget—"

It was her turn to cut him off as she followed his steps, smacking his arm down and away from my direction.

A smirk lifted my lips.

"I get to mess up sometimes!" she shouted. "I'm telling you, I was just distracted writing that letter and I—" Her eyes found mine. "I just forgot, alright? You're acting like a Goddessdamn child!"

Korven laughed sardonically. "Oh, *I'm* acting like a child? When you know how worried we've been for you here, and the one fucking thing, Morella—*the one fucking thing* you were supposed to add to every single letter, you just happened to forget? Do you know how panicked we've been? Seraphine practically pushed my ass out the Goddessdamn door to get to you as soon as your letter—"

I stepped forward casually, my hands sliding into my pockets. "You speak to the Queen of the Citrine Cliffs. You will apply respectful language when you discuss your matters with her."

"Oh, fuck off." His wings flung wide. "Who do you think taught her these words, hmm? She's my sister and this is how we speak to each other so—"

"And she is my—" I cleared my throat, adjusting my shoulders. "She is the queen of this kingdom and deserves your respect, regardless of what you've taught her."

He glanced back to Morella before turning his full attention on me. "Alright, King of the Citrine Cliffs," he said mockingly. He shoved his hands in his pockets, mimicking my stance. I was much larger than the Cursebringer, though his height only slightly fell beneath mine. "Let's discuss this civilly."

"Let's," I agreed.

"My most beloved sister here claims that you are not mistreating her. She also informs me that you do not know of the pact we made before I brought her here to join you in marriage. Which is at least *one* thing she's done right because she wasn't supposed to tell you."

"If Queen Morella was not to speak to me of this pact, then of course she would not. She is most loyal to the people she loves, which appears to be you, your wife, and daughter."

"You don't know her like I do," he grumbled.

"No, I should think that would be inappropriate."

"Oh, fucking hell," Morella muttered, followed by Fedir's snicker and Korven's tightly locked jaw.

"If you've forced your advances on my sister—"

"I have not," I interrupted.

He gave a curt nod. "Be thankful she has confirmed this."

I peered over his shoulder and ridiculously sized wings. "Thank you, Morella, for informing your most charming brother that all of my advances have indeed been met with vigor."

"This is *not* happening," she groaned and I returned my attention to Korven, doing little to hide the smugness in my chest.

He ignored it and continued. "Morella is to consume thistle nuts each day to keep her strength. She has done this since she was ten years old. I have ensured she has had access to them every day of her life since then, including enough supply to last her the entire three months of your marriage before she could leave and return home. Every one of her letters was to contain the words 'thistle nuts' in some capacity to ensure to myself and my wife that she was being treated well here in this,"—he waved a hand around the grand foyer—"overly bedazzled castle."

I huffed a laugh, nodding my understanding.

"However," he continued, "her last letter was short. Clipped, and very unlike my sister, and what do you think it was missing?"

I glanced at her as she chewed her lip, her arms folded across her chest. I raised a brow and her face scrunched in her admittance to me that she indeed had forgotten to add this little secret to her last letter.

"Forgive me," I sighed. "I'm afraid I know what distracted her so when she was last writing to her family."

Korven frowned, giving me a quizzical brow.

I smiled—all teeth—and said, "It was my bare chest, you see."

"Oh my fucking Goddess, Killian!" she yelled, storming to us.

Korven inched closer, his voice pure venom. "You think I give a shit if my sister finds you sexually appealing?"

Morella groaned again, stopping short.

He continued. "She can use you however she'd like—I really don't care. But her health, her mental well-being, and her strength—those are mine to care for. She is my family, I love her, and I'll be fucking Goddessdamned if she's mistreated in any way here in this kingdom or otherwise."

"We share this sentiment then," I replied. "She has not been mistreated even remotely as queen of this kingdom, nor in our marriage. Your concern is understandable, yet unnecessary. Your sister no longer needs thistle nuts. Her blood lacks the capacity to retain iron, and so, she now eats *fuilhe* and other iron-rich foods to keep her strength."

His dark eyes widened and he turned to his sister.

She sighed heavily, pinching the bridge of her nose. "*I've been trying to tell you.* I've been more than taken care of here. I'm stronger, Korven. The fuilhe is a blood meat they make from sheep. I practice flying each day and look—" She spread her wings across her back, the golden tips glinting as they rose high above her head.

Korven's face paled and his mouth parted. He walked slowly

to her side, stepping around her span of feathers, pinching parts of her bone, inspecting them in silence.

Morella's face beamed as her brother checked the adjustment, the balance, and the strength of her wings as he pushed down, trying to collapse them. Her strength held and she laughed lightly.

"I can fly much longer, too, in my shift," she said softly, grabbing her brother's hand.

"How long?" he asked.

"Almost an hour."

A gargled sob left his chest. "An hour?"

She nodded, grinning ear to ear. I'd never seen her light up like this. Her cheeks beamed as she took both of his hands. "I don't tire like I did before. I feel stronger. I feel...powerful. I was going to tell you, but I wanted you to see for yourself when you came to visit—as a surprise." She nodded to Fedir. "He figured out it was the iron in my blood."

Fedir held up both of his hands. "It wasn't me, Your Majesty. King Killian read through our medical books until the early hours of the morning, searching for what might be your condition. I only confirmed his findings and set about researching which foods you should eat."

Morella's eyes pierced me then. I hadn't told her it was me; I'd rather be left out of it.

Korven finally spoke again. "You've done this for my sister?"

I held her gaze, subduing my racing heart as she looked at me with...too much hope.

I nodded once, crossing my arms, unwilling to trust the steadiness of my voice.

The Cursebringer dropped her hands, storming the last few feet between us in a flash. I hadn't time to react as he reached up, pulling me into an embrace. He slapped my back heartily, his arms tight around my shoulders.

I didn't know what to do or how to respond.

"Thank you," he said. He squeezed tighter. "Thank you for doing what I could not."

My chest rumbled and I cleared my throat, my sanity hanging by a thread. I unclenched my arms, returning this unasked for hug, patting at his back gently.

I managed to reply, "You're welcome," before I caught Morella's eyes on me as she swallowed hard and let the tear fall down her cheek.

CHAPTER 27

Morella

"I STILL CAN'T BELIEVE IT," KORVEN MUTTERED AS WE sat atop the western tower roof, peering out into the setting sun.

I leaned my head on his shoulder as he wrapped an arm around me. "You didn't know what it was. No one knew."

"I should have researched somehow. I should have called for more physicians."

I shrugged. "You were helping raise me and had at least a dozen doctors poking at me since I could walk. No figured it out and it's not your fault or anyone's."

His voice went soft as he kissed the top of my head like he did when I was a child. "I'm sorry, Morella."

"Don't be." I squeezed his hand, a smile lifting my lips. "If my life hadn't been hard like it was, we couldn't be here now, like this. I'd be off doling out those odious curses and you'd be off in some random woman's bed instead of at home with your Seraphine and Avici."

"What if you had been happy as Cursebringer?"

I laughed. "You know I hate those curses. I cannot stand how our mother is still under hers, and what about Seraphine? You could have lost her to one. I'd rather be queen of a distant kingdom than do what you do, brother."

He shrugged. "It isn't so bad. And as for our mother…"

I lifted my head. "Have you heard from her?"

"No," he sighed. "Wherever she's gone, she hasn't sent word."

It had been almost a year without any news of where the Ravenfae Goddess had disappeared to. But this wasn't the first time she'd left the Brackish Wood. The last time, she returned seven months pregnant with me and no story to relay to her people or her son.

"I hope she's happy. Wherever she is."

"And you, Morella?" He pulled me back to his shoulder. "Are you happy here?"

Tears pricked my eyes, stinging in the truth that I didn't even consider denying. I sniffed, wiping my sleeve across my nose. "I love him, Korven," I murmured softly.

He squeezed my shoulders as if he already knew. As if he could reassure me that it was all right to love when that love was not returned.

Breathing a sigh, he said, "He cares for you. I can see that at least. Perhaps with more time—"

"We don't have time," I interrupted. "We have these three months and then it's over. He has said as much." I paused a moment, gathering what thoughts I was willing to reveal. "He does care, but…it doesn't seem to be enough for him to treat our marriage like I see it. Like how I know it could be."

"It's not like you to give up on what you want."

"No," I agreed. "It isn't. But there's more to it than I've told you."

He jerked back. "You're not in danger, are you?"

"Nothing like that. Have you met Céad?"

He shook his head. "Mother has mentioned her once or twice. She's not…all there. Madness has taken her along with her obsession for change."

"Well, Killian made a bargain with her. A long time ago. And I'm trying to help him fulfill it."

He chuckled. "The fae Goddess bargain, eh? Do you think it can be fulfilled?"

"Yes," I said with confidence. "I do. I know I can help him."

"Then I don't see why you'd give up on what you could have here. You've been imagining this life for years and here it is." He gestured to the sea of rolling green hills ahead of us, turning golden in the setting sun. "If our mother taught us anything, it's to take what we want. What we need. Regardless of the obstacles."

I took a deep breath, my lungs filling with the breeze off the Citrine Cliffs in the distance. I knew what I wanted. I knew Killian wanted at least some of those same things, too. It was time to jump and risk everything we'd had so far, even if it seemed like no more than a frayed thread between us.

"Thank you, Korven," I sighed.

"You're welcome, Little Fungi."

I laughed heartily, rising to my feet, ready to shift and say my last goodbye to him before he left to explain to Seraphine what happened. "I haven't heard that in a very long time."

He brought me into a hug once more, resting his chin on my head. "That's what older brothers do. They never let you forget you still have a home and a history of where you came from."

BY THE TIME I STEPPED BACK INTO OUR ROOM, NIGHT had fallen and the fireplace roared, soothing away the autumn chill.

My husband sat by the fire and from his position alone, I sensed the thinly-held control in the stiffness of his body. Without turning to greet me, he asked, "Is the Cursebringer gone?"

My stomach dropped at his tone. "Yes."

He nodded and I crept forward, setting three spools of woven golden thread I'd just finished on the small desk. Keeping my gift held tightly to my chest, I swallowed hard and joined him at the chairs by the fire. He was sitting back, legs sprawled open, face resting on one hand as he watched my every move.

I cleared my throat, adjusting my burgundy skirts and kicking off my shoes, folding my legs up underneath me on the chair. "I'm sorry," I began, "for the sudden appearance of my brother today."

"He loves you," he mumbled. "You should not be sorry for that."

I nodded. "Korven has always been overly protective of me. My lack of strength and...my condition only fueled that fire over the years."

"He took your birthright."

"No," I amended. "He saved me from failing at the duty of the heir to the Ravenfae Goddess. I could not have succeeded as Cursebringer, nor did I want the job."

He paused, still holding onto that tight control. "And now you're here."

"And now, I'm here," I echoed. I gently unfolded his midnight blue coat—the one I'd stolen from his wardrobe. "I have something for you." Holding up the embroidered cuffs, I explained, "I've added some new details to this one. Wheat, to represent our bargain, and a threaded line that connects back to itself to represent our rings of marriage."

His deep blue eyes narrowed and I backtracked quickly. "It's just a pretty design and I wanted to find a way to thank you for what you've done for me these past six weeks." I dared looking up. "Will you wear it for me?"

Something slipped in his face, but he caught it quickly, rising in silence to meet me as I held the sleeves out so he could slip his arms through. He adjusted the jacket, fixing the cuffs and tracing his fingers over the intricate design.

"You have many talents, Goldling," he mumbled and I beamed, sticking close to his chest as I adjusted his shirt underneath.

"This suits you perfectly," I cooed, patting down the lapel.

"You think me handsome, Moh Dhóches?"

I hummed. "No, my king."

His brows rose and I laughed. "I think you too beautiful for such a common word. I think of you as a brilliant sun, heating every room you walk into. I think you to be fuckable in every sense of the word."

His hand shot forward, grabbing the underside of my chin and lifting my head to meet his eyes. "This *mouth* on you," he gritted, pulling me closer still with a hand against the small of my back.

"Yes," I breathed in a heated smile. "This *mouth* on me."

His eyes darted to my lips as they parted, begging for him to kiss me. Instead, his hand slid slowly down my neck and he released my back entirely. "Thank you, Morella. This jacket exceeds anything it was before you laid your hands upon it."

I refused to move. "Is that all you'll say?" I whispered.

"I have nothing more to discuss."

I pulled him closer, my anger rising. "Well, I do. I have more to discuss with you."

He pulled my hands away with heartbreaking tenderness and backed towards the study door. "I cannot do this."

"Do what?" I shouted, following him.

"Our bargain still stands and I have nothing left to teach you except Céaduah. You may join me in my study in an hour if you wish to keep to your lesson tonight. If you don't, I would not find fault in your—"

"Don't do this," I begged, darting around his large frame and blocking the study door. "Don't turn away again. Don't leave just because you can't face what's so clear between us, Killian."

He glared at me, folding his arms. "We've been contracted into this marriage and made a bargain. There is nothing more—"

I cut him off again. "Liar."

His jaw clamped tight before he muttered, "Move from this door, Morella."

"Not until you admit you love me."

Shock lit his features and he dropped his arms. I continued with ferocity, my heart pounding and pleading. "Not until you tell me that I am not the only one in this marriage who has fallen because I love you, Killian. And I *need* you, Killian. And I will be here—two weeks from now, five months, seven years—I don't care how long you've planned for our marriage—for me, it's forever. For me, it's the only marriage I'll know and you are the husband I want." My voice finally cracked, but I swallowed it down, pushing away from the door and padding softly to him. "You are the husband I was fated to marry, and I'm tired of keeping this distance between us."

I met his chest with mine, breathing in the scent of him and pressing my hands to his shirt. "It doesn't have to be the way it's been."

He grabbed my wrists in one hand, holding them away from his body. "It does," he gritted.

"Why?"

"Because anything more..." He stopped, shaking his head. His face calmed, adopting that stony facade I was sick of seeing. "I have work left to do. Study if you wish. You may practice with me in an hour, as I said."

With a cold stare, he gently pulled me aside, opening the yellow door.

He was leaving me. Regardless of what I'd confessed and what I claimed to know of his own feelings, he hadn't acknowledged them at all.

In a daze I stepped back, unfurling my wings. My mind swirled with everything he'd said, with every way he'd looked at me, grumbled at me...kissed me, and I tried to piece together where I'd gone wrong.

I thought he loved me.

He'd never said it, but I thought I knew...

"What are you doing?" His voice snapped my attention back to him, and I was startled to find myself backing up to the large windows near his bed. I blinked a few times, shaking my head and my wings stretched further.

The room was suddenly too hot—too small and heavy with the weight of the truth in the distance between us; I was not going to keep my husband.

"Morella—" he began.

"I need air," I gulped, breathing hard and reaching behind me for the window latch.

"Do not leave," he called, crossing the room in great, hurried strides, but I couldn't let him get to me. I couldn't let him reach me or—Goddess forbid—*touch* me only for me to fall apart and beg—beg for him to love me like I loved him.

I shook my head some more, managing the latch and the window flew open, blowing the curtains out into the night. "I just need some...air."

"Stop!" he yelled, his hand reaching for me just as I shifted and flew out the window, nothing more than a dim blur of golden feathers on the wind.

CHAPTER 28

Killian

SHE TOLD ME SHE LOVED ME.

And I hadn't said a Goddessdamn meaningful thing in return.

If Céad was coming to kill me in six weeks, I fucking deserved it.

CHAPTER 29

Morella

I FLEW FOR MILES.

I didn't know where I was going, or what I'd do when I got there, but I flew. I realized at least an hour had passed when the moon was full in the sky above me. Tired, I soared on the wind toward the lights of the town ahead of me. I'd managed to keep my thoughts blurred and my mind clear of the heartbreak, but as I landed in an alleyway and shifted back to Ravenfae, everything came crashing down.

I fell to my knees in a dirty puddle, shivering and barefoot—a mess of a queen, desperately trying to hold in broken sobs amidst the voices coming from the bustling tavern across the cobbled road.

I didn't know which town I'd landed in or how I was going to find a place to rest until my strength returned. I had no money, no proof I was Queen of the Citrine Cliffs, and only just enough Céaduah to possibly get me through a conversation.

I recognized the language as I tried to pull my pathetic self together and gather the courage to ask for help at the tavern. I picked myself up, brushing off what filth I could and took a deep breath. I didn't know what I'd do after the night was over, but finding a place to rest was forced to the forefront of my mind.

It's why I didn't notice the men.

Three Changelingfae stepped out from a dark alcove I hadn't seen when I'd landed. They blocked my way out of the alley and one of them stepped forward. "Nah rud be brèagha a ayn?"

I shivered hard, understanding most of what he'd said.

Aren't you a pretty little thing?

I braced my feet, knowing I didn't have the strength to shift again and fly away.

"Che ehch fay ar fobh, eun brèagha."

No need to leave, pretty bird.

His voice slurred and his friends laughed, staggering in their drunken stupors towards me. I took it as an opening, unfurling my wings and jumping into the air, stumbling in the lack of space in the alleyway, but managing to fly over their heads. Their hands reached for me, but missed and I tumbled back to the ground, falling slightly to my knees before I could pick myself back up and run.

I didn't see the fourth as he grabbed hold of my wing and pulled me down to the ground. "Be eun brèagha."

Pretty little bird.

His breath reeked of ale and I kicked him right in his teeth, fumbling to my feet and breaking into a run. I passed the tavern and the closed shops, my footfall slapping against the hard bricks, breaking open my skin.

"Cidech mi!" I screamed, pleading for anyone to help as I was toppled by one of them, falling onto the cold stone of a bridge over a rushing river. His hand covered my mouth next as he pinned me. I gagged and kicked, flailing my fists in all the soft places on his body, earning a hard grunt and curse as he fell off me.

My brother had taught me hand-to-hand combat and I'd taught him how to knit. One of these skills was more valuable to a lone woman in Revelry.

I kicked his face while he was down, bracing myself for the

next one as he launched at me, attempting to grab my arms. I ducked, earning another curse as I punched at the bend of his knees, causing him to topple forward. Already drunk and stumbling, he landed on the stone wall of the bridge and I helped him right over.

His scream lit the night air before there was a splash and the third man rushed to the railing, screaming his name.

"Chan ur ha sàm!"

He can't swim!

I laughed, manically, wiping my hair off my face. "Am chrò dhuinn ficainn an ur dhut?"

Should we see if you can?

He cursed in a word I'd not yet learned, but assumed was something foul, and lunged, fingers curled and face mad with rage.

He dropped dead before I could ready a stance to toss him over the side as well. A knife protruded from his spine, glinting in the moonlight.

I gasped, stepping back and tripping over the first one still sobbing on the ground with a broken nose, blood gushing onto the stone. Another knife flew through the air, slicing into his neck in the cleanest throw I'd ever seen.

I blinked in confusion as Killian raced across the bridge, two more knives already in hand, his eyes piercing mine as he reached the bodies. Fedir was only a few steps behind, dragging the fourth, pathetic whimpers coming from the last of the men who'd assaulted me, planning for worse.

"Are you hurt?" Killian asked, his eyes roaming over my body in assessment.

"Not really," I replied, ignoring the sting of cuts on my feet.

He nodded in silence, taking the knife from the man's back and tossing him over the side of the bridge. As if the corpse was no more than a pillow, he picked up the next, flinging it into the river as well. We stared at each other as we heard the splash of the third Changelingfae we'd killed tonight.

"One more," Fedir called, tossing forward the last of my attackers. He hit the stones in a scream of pain, his shoulder popped out of its socket.

Killian lifted him with ease, tossing him over the side to join the others in a watery grave. He held his hand out to me in silence and I took it, the night suddenly too quiet. He led me to a wooden lamppost at the end of the bridge, Fedir following just close enough to touch Killian's shoulder before we shifted through the wood.

A tavern booth.

A stack of logs.

A grove of trees and then we were back, shifting out of our bedroom door, warm and familiar.

I took a few weak steps, inhaling sharply on my cut feet before I fell to the floor.

"Your Majesty!" Fedir cried, instantly at my feet, surveying the damage. "You'll need these washed and bandaged. Are you hurt anywhere else?"

I shook my head.

"Leave, Fedir." Killian slid out of his jacket, surprisingly free of blood.

The captain ignored him, continuing. "You might be sore in the morning. We arrived just as you tossed that piece of shit into the river. Once Killian found me, we followed you through the fields beneath the trees. You were easy enough to spot with your golden feathers. When you fell from the sky, it took us a minute to figure out exactly where you landed. But we followed your shouts." He lifted my foot, dabbing at the blood with a handkerchief. "Glad to see our queen can hold her own in a fight."

I hissed as he pulled a rock from the cut.

He grimaced. "Sorry."

"Fedir, go," Killian ordered, rolling up the cuffs of his sleeves and jerking his head toward the door.

Fedir ignored him again, lifting my other foot and inspecting the lesser cuts. "I have an ointment that can help your healing, but your sister's might be—"

"Get the fuck out!" Killian snapped.

"Not until I'm done," Fedir growled.

"I order you out of this room, Captain!"

Fedir flashed to his feet, meeting Killian in a rage. "She is my *queen!*"

"SHE IS MY *WIFE!*"

The air left my lungs and my chin trembled as I looked upon them both. Fedir stepped back instantly, nodding slowly. He huffed a short laugh. "About fucking time." Bowing to me as I sat on the floor, he said, "I'll check on you in the morning." He slapped Killian's shoulder as he left, softly closing the carved wooden door behind him.

Killian lowered himself to the floor, assessing me with a murderous look. "Did they touch you?"

I shook my head. "Not like that. But—" I bit my lips together, gathering courage. "But they would have if you hadn't found me."

He murmured softly, "Are you alright, Moh Dhóches?"

I gave him a small smile. "Yes. With you."

His lashes fluttered at my words before he offered his hands, lifting me as I took them. He helped me to the chair by the fire, adding, "Sit. Do not move."

I nodded obediently and he left through the bathing room door, returning shortly with a stool and small basin of steaming water.

He sat, barely fitting on the stool as he bent, picking up my ankle and gently lowering my foot into the heat. I gripped the sides of the chair but didn't make a sound, even through the sharp sting.

He took a deep breath and began to speak. "The first woman I ever loved, Céad murdered in our bed."

I stilled as he washed, his large hands so delicate and gentle tracing over my wounds.

"Her name was Claragh and we were barely twenty-two. I'd just become king and had years left in the bargain before she needed to discover my name, so she never even tried." He patted my foot dry, unfolding a towel and revealing a jar of Seraphine's blue healing salve and strips of cloth. As he added the ointment, he continued. "We were young and in love. Nothing could stand in our way and our future was bright. I woke in her bed one morning and I thought she was still asleep." He began to wrap my foot gently, tying the ends of the cloth together. "It took me ten minutes of lying next to her before I realized something was wrong."

He set my foot on the floor and picked up the next. "Hanreigh came into my life a year later. She was the daughter of a shepherd I visited often as we experimented with the moss from the Brackish Wood. I slept with her once and found her dead the next morning."

I swallowed, a single tear flowing down my cheek. "How did she—"

He looked up. "Céad cut their throats. I heard the madness in her laughter upon each discovery of their bodies."

He dipped my foot into the water, beginning again. "Two years later, I thought that if I hid Sorcha, she'd discover my name and fulfilling the bargain would mean Céad could no longer haunt me, and my power would return." Patting my foot dry, he began the same treatment, his voice falling. "We were careful, Morella. We snuck around, meeting at inns or her family's estate. We planned our future in private, but it wasn't until we slept together that Céad came." He nodded toward his bed. "I found her there one morning, her blood pooled in the sheets, her body cold as I tore the blankets back to see that I had caused yet another woman's death."

He finished wrapping my foot and sighed. "Another woman I loved."

He dipped the rag into the water, lifting my muddy skirts to my knees and began washing my legs, splattered in filth.

"I didn't know," I said softly. "That the other Changelingfae who were to discover your name...were your lovers."

He nodded. "When you arrived, I was angry. I'd forged our contract so many years before, certain you'd get yourself out of it." His strokes were light along my skin, brushing away what grime was left. "And then you showed up to our wedding in red." His eyes lifted and he dropped the rag. "I hated the color. I couldn't see it and not think of blood-stained sheets...until I saw you."

My lips trembled and a half sob, half laugh came from my chest.

"You were so beautiful and free. I knew right then that I couldn't keep you. I couldn't risk even knowing you. I didn't trust your life with my foolish heart." He shook his head and laughed. "When you pulled your trunk into this room that night, I thought you were mad. I should have turned you away. I know I should have forced you back to your room, but I couldn't. A stronger man would have, Morella, because I knew what you were doing. I saw that you wanted a marriage. You wanted to fall in love and I should have stopped you right then. Before I discovered more about you. Before I memorized your smile—before I knew the little things. What you like on your toasted bread, what your steps sound like as you cross barefoot through a room...what curse words you prefer when you're angry or making a point."

He dried my legs and chuckled. "And you're right. I am a liar. I've been lying to you for weeks. I do love your kiss on my head each morning as you join me for breakfast. I do love listening to your songs as you spin, and I love waiting for the sound of your steps down the stairs." He pounded his chest. "It grips me here every time I hear them. I love irritating you, just so I can hear what you'll say. I love your clever thinking and ease into your Changelingfae heritage and the language of your people. I love teaching you. Touching you. Tasting you. But your kisses, Morella, those I love most. Each day I've lied, but each night I've been the most selfish of men. Because those are my truth. But I cannot have them. I cannot love you as I want just to lose you to her."

"Killian," I whispered, reaching out, touching his cheek and wiping the tear I found there. "Moh Dhóches," I added, "I didn't know it was Céad. I didn't know it was your lovers she killed. If you'd have just told me, you'd know by now that she cannot hurt me."

"She can." He hung his head, pinching the bridge of his nose. "She will."

"No," I urged, lifting his head in my hands. "A Goddess of the Veil cannot hurt the child of another."

He frowned, his voice firm. "Morella, she has killed every woman I've loved after we shared a bed."

"No, dammit, *listen*. The Goddesses—they have a bargain together. *'None will harm one and none will harm any with the blood of the other.'* They made this pact to ensure their bloodlines would live on forever." I smiled softly, brushing my thumb across his cheek. "She cannot hurt me, Killian. She cannot take me away from you."

Pain shifted across his face. "What are you saying exactly?"

"I'm saying that you are free to love me as your wife. *She cannot kill me, Killian.*" I kissed his lips softly, reassuring, "She cannot."

He swallowed hard. "She'll find a way," he whispered. "She'll take you from me somehow."

"*Listen to me*," I ordered, my voice steady between us. "If she herself harmed me or orchestrated such a thing, she would perish. The pact the Goddesses made is strong. Their combined power fuels it. It's part of why there are not many children of the Goddesses. They do not fear their children's death, for their children are Goddessblessed by each of the thirteen."

He closed his eyes and I felt the weight of the fear he carried roll off him as his shoulders slumped. His arms wrapped around my waist and I brought his head to my chest. "She cannot hurt me, Moh Geràdah. She cannot take me from you."

"I've been so afraid," he whispered. "I can't just let that fear go. I...I don't know how."

I ran my fingers through his hair. "It will take time. It will take trust. But we have everything we need right here. I love you. I want you. I'll do what it takes to have all of you. *All* of you, Killian. Give me your fears and I shall soothe them away." I kissed the top of his head. "Give me your pain and I shall help you heal." I lifted his chin, watching him break—all reservations gone in an instant and I smiled with relief in my heart. "Give me your nightmares and I shall weave you new dreams."

"*Morella*," he breathed, lifting himself to kiss me, pulling me out of the chair and into his arms. I wrapped my legs around him as he held me, carrying me to my bed and setting me on top of the sheets.

"Are you sure you're alright?" he whispered as I lifted his shirt up over his head, feeling my way down his arms.

"Yes," I answered breathlessly, taking more kisses from his mouth. "I want you in this bed." I pulled my dress down my shoulders, shivering at the heat of those eyes on my bare skin. "If you're ready to stay with me." I shimmied out of my soiled gown, naked and baring my heart before him. "But if you're not ready to—"

"Lie back, Moh Dhóches."

I obeyed immediately, melting in the grip of his hands wrapping around my thighs as he pushed my legs apart, staring at me.

"The only good dreams I've had since you arrived were of this." He lowered himself onto the bed, smoothing his cheek across the skin of my thigh, kissing right where he had that first night we'd done this weeks ago.

He opened his mouth, and I moaned in the heat of his tongue tracing over me. "I've pleasured myself to this, Morella." Another kiss, another long drag of his lips. "And yes, I've imagined your mouth replacing my hand."

I watched him lick and suck his way across my clit and when he added his fingers, curving them up to that place he'd once found, I cried out, begging for all of it.

"There's so much more to teach you," he said, replacing his mouth with his thumb. "And you're such a quick learner, Moh Dhóches."

"Please," I begged, "teach me more."

He withdrew himself and I whimpered, replacing his hand with my own. Watching in growing hunger, he stepped out of his pants, curling his hand around his stiff cock. I slipped two fingers inside myself, finding that place as he taught me and moaning, letting my head fall back onto the pillow.

He knelt on the bed, taking my fingers and bringing them to my mouth. "Taste it, Morella. Taste how good and ready you are for me." I closed my eyes, licking over my fingers and he groaned. "Good girl. You listen so well, Goldling."

I reached out, pulling his hand away and stroking his hard length. "Please, Killian," I begged, my other hand coaxing him closer, pulling him down on top of me.

His lips met mine as his hand roamed over my chest. He trailed down my neck, reaching the peak of my breast and pulled a nipple into his mouth, swirling his tongue in a circular motion, coaxing even more begging from my lips.

He readied his cock, leaving just the head at my entrance. Brushing my hair back from my face, he whispered, "What is my name, Morella?"

"I-I don't know," I breathed. My hips lifted, pushing more of him into me.

Air left his lungs quickly and he shook his head. "You do. You do know it. Intimately."

"I can't—"

"You can," he finished, kissing me hard and slipping in a little more.

"What is my name, Goldling?"

"I don't know, Killian, please!" I wriggled beneath him, his cock only barely inside me, but I needed all of him. I needed to feel all of my husband, filling me completely.

"You do," he added, slipping further inside. "You do, Moh Dhóches."

A little further and he sucked air between his teeth.

"Moh Geràdah."

My love.

I shrieked as he slipped in further, breathing hard, going slow, helping me stretch over him.

"Moh Bheren."

My wife.

I gasped as he withdrew, sliding back in instantly. "Lorgair mi d' arin, debheren."

I will find your name, husband.

"Agus bid mi a' fuck mar a brehb tu."

And I will scream it as you fuck me.

A laugh, deep and low, came between us. He rose onto his knees, digging his hands into my hips and holding me steady. He began to thrust, slow at first, letting my body adjust until his cock hit that place inside of me and I cried out.

"There," he cooed. "Look at you, taking me so perfectly. I knew you would."

His body picked up speed and I struggled to stay with him, losing myself into mindless pleasure as he fucked me faster and faster, each thrust sending me further into moans and cries of pleading for more.

"That's it," he growled. "Open up all the way for me, wife."

I did as he instructed, widening my hips, gripping his forearms. "Like this?" I breathed in reply.

"Perfect," his face tightened as I felt myself letting go, squeezing his cock as my release began to ripple through my body.

He moaned, and bent forward, hovering over me, taking my mouth with his. "So fucking perfect," he breathed before pressing his tongue to mine as the rest of my body shuddered, holding him as close as I could.

"*Morella*," he gasped, pumping hard, extending my own release into something sharper, bringing me to clarity. "*Morella*," he called again, slowing, breathing heavily, both of us completely spent.

I wrapped my arms around his back, keeping him with me, kissing him deeply.

As our lips parted, he stared into my eyes. I saw the turmoil there. I saw the love.

"No," I reassured. "This wasn't a mistake. You did nothing wrong. I will be right here with you in the morning and the morning after that. I am safe. You will not lose me."

He brushed his hand across my cheek. "I love you."

I nodded, sliding my hand over his, grinning like a fool. "I feel it, husband. I love you, too."

CHAPTER 30

Killian

MORELLA SLEPT THROUGH THE NIGHT.

Her breathing came deep and peaceful, even after all she'd been through.

I knew because I was there for all of it—awake and waiting.

Waiting for a Goddess who did not come.

When morning broke, still, I waited.

I did not take rest because I could not lose her.

When she stirred, stretching and moaning in a contented sigh, I kissed her softly, needing more from her—reassuring myself that dawn had come and she was safe.

As I moved in her again, filling her with all of me, praising her in soft whispers, I felt the first prickle of hope enter the blood in my veins. As she cursed in the filthiest of words, begging for more, harder, faster, I gave it all.

I'd keep giving it all because it was over for me.

Whatever happened in six weeks, it was out of my hands and into hers.

I gave her everything she begged for, taking her hand and kissing the tips of her fingers.

My fate couldn't have landed in the hands of a more perfect wife.

And in whatever time we had left together, I'd make sure she knew it.

"Willow to seed,
How does the earth sing,
When silver moon's a changin'?
How does the sky,
Whisper so nigh,
When silver moon's a changin'?"

MY EYES DRIFTED AS MY WIFE SANG SOFTLY IN THE western tower, spinning her straw into gold. I jerked my head up, catching her warm smile as she continued her song. The wheel spun in a blur as thread wound over her third spool.

I wouldn't wait for her at the bottom of the stairs any longer. Indeed, I had followed her around all morning, never letting her out of my sight. She allowed it, though I had the feeling she wouldn't give into my fears for long.

Her humming continued and I closed my eyes just for a moment as I leaned against the door to the room. The world buzzed and my bones ached from a full day without rest.

I'd made love to my wife twice in that time and as memories of filling her roamed through my thoughts, I was able to stay awake, my blood heating again for what I'd deprived myself of for so long.

"Moh Dhóches." The sound of her sweet voice brought me back to the present. She had silently found her way to me and stood on the tips of her toes, almost reaching my mouth with hers.

Like a moth to flame, I leaned in, taking her lips to mine, pulling her up to rid the distance between us.

Had I a future, this would be it. There, in a tower room, with morning winter sun pouring through the window in a dim haze while my wife pressed her body to mine, her hands wandering low down my chest.

She left my lips, sliding her mouth to my neck, leaving trails of kisses over the hollow of my throat. My chest rumbled with an unbidden sound and she snickered. "I've fulfilled my end of the bargain for the day, husband. What of yours?"

"You wish me to kiss you goodnight?"

Her hand found the band of my pants and her fingers slipped inside. "I wish you to kiss me until it is night and I can't take anymore."

I hissed in a breath as her hand found me, hard and aching for her again.

"*Furich mi*," I murmured, setting my head back against the door as she continued her strokes.

"Furich mi?" she asked. "What is that?"

"It's your lesson for today, Goldling." I pulled her closer, backing us into the door where I shifted us through, landing out of her oak dressing screen and straight onto her bed—to hell with walking across the room. We didn't have time for it.

I kissed her hard, pulling up the skirts of her dress, finding her wet and ready to take me. I groaned into her mouth and mumbled on her lips, "It means 'fuck me' and it's all I want to hear for the next hour."

"The next *hour*?" she cried, gasping when I yanked down her dress and took her nipple into my mouth. "Surely you don't have enough energy for that."

I hummed, moving lower, pulling down the rest of her gown as I went until my face was between her legs. I looked up at her as I licked my way across her clit.

"Your lesson, Goldling," I mumbled, filling my mouth with her in the next breath.

"Tha mi a iardh ot furich mi."

I want you to fuck me.

"Tha mi a iradh ot goal mi."

I want you to love me.

"Tha mi a iradh or caal còre riam nar leadh a uile oiche."

I want you to sleep with me in our bed every night.

"Orson a còrrdb de ar beha."

For the rest of our lives.

I was plunging into her a moment later, pulling her body to sit up with mine because she didn't get to say that if I wasn't inside her, dragging that breathless whimper from her chest as my dick hit just right. "Nìrr mi ubh, Moh Dhóches," I breathed into her skin, lifting her and slamming her back down with no more gentle patience.

I will, my fate.

"*Furich mi! Furich mi!*" she cried, grinding her hips in time with my thrusts.

I would. Goddess, I would every day and night until my very last, I would.

CHAPTER 31

Morella

KILLIAN'S BODY, WARM, BUT HEAVY, SPRAWLED ACROSS my chest as he finally slept. I squirmed, adjusting my wings and lifting my head with a pillow as he passed out entirely. I didn't think he'd meant to fall asleep.

The stubborn ass was planning to stay awake forever, just waiting for Céad to come slice my throat and take me from him for good. I smoothed his red hair back from his face, admiring the few freckles across his cheeks and neck. I grinned like a fool in love because this was what I'd wanted, what I'd waited for and convinced him we could have together.

Kissing his hair, I adjusted him further, gently lifting his head to rest below my breasts so I could actually breathe. I reached for the thirteenth book in the Language of the Changelingfae series and opened to my current place, held for me by a long strip of crimson ribbon.

This final volume was an assortment of many subjects. It taught the Céaduah names for different animals in Revelry, climates, and weather systems. I was skimming over these words carefully, looking for anything that could relate to Killian. I'd said so many words at the edge of that cliff on so many chilled mornings—combinations of things that could lead to just one correct pronunciation of his true name.

I knew it was there—somewhere between the pages of those books was the key I needed to save my sister from a human death and my husband from losing his powers forever.

I absently stroked my fingers through his hair, covering us both before allowing Alista into our room to deliver two bowls of mutton stew and fresh baked bread. She took one look at our position and grinned with a knowing smirk, backing out of the room quietly. I heard her insistence in the hall, telling Fedir we were occupied and he'd have to wait to check on the state of my wounds.

All was as it should be, but the nagging in my head would not leave. I had a task and I had to focus. I loved my husband, and he loved me, and now was the time to prove how clever his wife truly was.

My stomach gurgled and I glanced longingly at the bowls of stew, but I wasn't ready to wake him up just yet. I flipped to the next chapter and gasped at the footnote of the illustrations.

Morelli.

Mushrooms of all shapes and sizes littered the page, each with colorful details and defining features written in common and Céaduah.

Morelli.

Of *course.*

My name meant mushroom. Our mother had told Korven and me this, but we never bothered asking in which language or even *why*. Instead, he nicknamed me "Little Fungi," bringing out the moniker when I did something he found particularly humorous because who names their daughter after such a thing?

I held in my squeal, kicking my feet and covering my mouth.

This was it. Killian said I had all I needed to guess his name. He said I knew it. Intimately. He must have meant because it was a variation of my own.

I took a deep breath, leaning down to kiss the top of his head again and again. He stirred, but I soothed him back to sleep. I wouldn't be able to say his true name until morning anyway and it was best I kept it to myself. I could just see it—in the morning, we'd be ready. I'd shout his name across the valley below us and his power would return. Maybe Céad would finally show her face and congratulate us both. Maybe we'd shift right then, finding ourselves in front of Seraphine and Korven's door and he'd transform her into fae. Forestfae, I'd imagine, considering her upbringing and considering his own.

If Seraphine was Forestfae, she'd be able to shift through the trees and travel would be trivial for visits. They could arrive for solstices and birthdays. I breathed a sigh. I'd never miss one of my niece's birthdays. Ever. They could bring her for visits, they could drop her off and Killian and I could keep her here, giving Korven and Seraphine time to themselves. And when Killian and I had our own children, we could—

"What has you smiling like that, Moh Dhóches?"

His voice was gravelly as he blinked up at me, head still resting on my belly.

I bit my lip in my grin, shaking my head. "Shhh. Sleep, husband. I'll tell you in the morning."

CHAPTER 32

Killian

My wife hummed in excitement—like I'd never seen before, she bloomed in smiles as we readied in the early hours before dawn, headed to the cliffside. I suspected I knew why but I wouldn't allow myself too much hope. Hope was the first step to disappointment.

I asked if she was ready and she jumped into my arms, kissing me hard, like we had more time to explore than we did. I held her close, backing up into the door carved in forests and moss and mushrooms. We shifted together just like that, our mouths pressed tight, my arms wrapped around her as we left the line of trees before the Citrine Cliffs, the sun already beginning her glint across the crystals embedded into the rocky hills.

"I love you," she whispered and then left my arms, gathering her saffron gold skirts in her hands and half running, half flying to the sharp edge. I followed as fast as I could, but after all of her strengthening, I had to admit, she was quicker than me now.

I arrived just after her before the sun hit that line I stayed behind and I heard her deep intake of breath before she bellowed across the cliffs.

"MORELLI!"

The Céaduah word for *mushroom* echoed throughout the

canyon, disturbing the peaceful morning with what I could only name as my wife's brilliance.

I shoved my hands in my pocket, tears pricking in my eyes as I swallowed hard, biting back the lump in my throat, overcome with how perfect she was for me.

Goddessdamn me, I'd never love another.

She stilled, tilting her head and glancing back at me. Then, several times more, she repeated the word, changing the pronunciation slightly each time, waiting for something to happen—some glorious sign that she'd done what no other could.

When it was clear she had failed, that same disappointing betrayal of hope hit her, and she sank to the ground, folding her legs and hanging her head in her hands.

I crossed the line, letting the creeping sun rise on my face, not giving a damn about waiting for the full brilliance of dawn. I sat behind her, placing her on my lap and wrapping my arms around her shaking body.

"I-I thought I had it," she whimpered, turning and falling into my chest. "I thought because you said I have everything I need and that I know your name intimately, that I had found it." She wiped her nose on my shirt and I pressed her closer. "Morella is a feminine take on mushroom and I just…"

"Morella," I began, sweeping a hand over her hair. "My Goldling, I thank whatever Goddess it was who tethered us together because you are my match. My partner. My fate, and this brilliant mind of yours is what I love most." I kissed her gently. "You still have time—"

"Five weeks, Killian!" she burst angrily. "Little more than a month, my sister will die in what? Forty years? If she's lucky to even make it that far?" Sobs wracked her again. "And you? You'll just have to live like this. Céad could take all of your magic if she wanted without your bargain. If I fail, she could banish you or steal you from me and I can't—"

"Shh," I cooed, pulling her back into my arms. My chest

ached. She hadn't guessed that Céad would do far worse than that. "We have time, Moh Dhóches. We have time."

She lifted her head once more, fire in her golden eyes, more brilliant than the morning's rays as they glinted off the citrine embedded in the cliffside. "I *will* do this, Killian. I know it. I will save both of you."

"I believe you, Goldling," I whispered back, wiping her cheek. "I believe you."

CHAPTER 33

Morella

THE CASTLE HUMMED WITH AN UNEASE THAT DRIFTED through the halls. I tasted it in the food. I heard it in the hushed whispers. Something was changing and the Changelingfae of the Citrine Cliffs were aware of its looming presence.

I woke each morning before dawn, tangled with Killian. We would shift to the cliffside and I'd rattle off every possible fucking thing I could think of to be his name. He'd pace behind me, smile, and pull me to him as the sun hit his cheeks and hair, only to shift me back to our bed where he'd make love to me soft and gentle, whispering my praises and loving me as I was meant to be loved.

But I was fucking livid.

I didn't even spin anymore, keeping a tally in my journal of all the golden thread I owed him. I read books until my eyes blurred. I practiced my pronunciation until my voice was nothing more than a hoarse rasp. Alista brought me books she found around the castle that might help. Any time she discovered one written in Céaduah, it would show up in our room along with a hot cup of lemon honey tea.

Killian didn't say anything about the state of our room. Books open to random pages, ink spilled near the fireplace, and my dresses tossed about onto every surface—it looked like a storm had ravaged its way through.

I didn't have time to feel guilty about it, though.

I didn't have time to breathe, or eat, or think about anything other than his name.

His name, his name, his name. For weeks, I became obsessed with his name.

The cruel disappointment at my discovery of Morelli, only to find that I was wrong, consumed me, nagging at the back of my head that I would surely fail. That if I hadn't found it by now, I never would.

He found me deep in the stacks of the Citrine Library on the night before my last morning of attempts at his name. Early winter's chill bit through my loose shawl, only fueling my desperation to look harder, search wiser, and do the one thing I'd been tasked to do.

"Tig a laig, Goldling."

Come to bed, Goldling.

"Lig lem du bhalhadh."

Let me warm you.

"Lig lem gaol a torth."

Let me love you.

I pulled at the budding tears in my eyes, wiping them with a dirty sleeve and returning to the top shelf. "I can't," I explained, shoving my journal into his hands. "This is all I have. Ten potential names. And they're the least likely yet."

He took the book, his eyes flickering quickly over my messy scrawl. Closing it gently, he took my hand. "They're perfect, Goldling. You're done for the night." He tugged on me again, sweeping my body to his. "Tonight I get all of you to myself. No dusty books to read, no messes to wipe clean that you've left behind."

"Sorry," I burst.

He kissed my forehead. "You've done beautifully, Morella,

My Goldling, and I would not trade the last three months for anything."

I fell into him, sighing deep into his chest. "Not even your power re—"

"Not for anything." He pulled on my chin, forcing me to look into his eyes cut like gems, glistening with unshed tears. "Do you hear me, Moh Dhóches?"

I nodded, my chin trembling.

"Good," he answered. "Now let's leave this place. I have much worshipping to do before the night is through."

He led us up the winding stair and shifted us through the door, landing in our room where Fedir waited. The captain rose quickly from my fireplace chair but Killian did not seem surprised to see him.

"It's done?" Killian asked.

Fedir's jaw clamped shut and his eyes darted to me briefly. "As you've asked of me, my king."

"Good," Killian mumbled. "You may leave, Captain."

Fedir stayed put, a silent conversation happening right before my eyes between the two of them. Too exhausted to be nosey, I headed to the bathing room to prepare myself for a short sleep before I planned to wake again and head to the library. I'd stay there all night, and when the sun peeked in the sky, I'd be at the cliffside, reading from the Goddessdamn books themselves if I had to.

When I left the bathing chamber, they were arguing in hardly contained whispers.

"I don't care about your morals, Captain," Killian said.

"And what of the morals of your friend?" Fedir snapped back, catching Killian off-guard.

Killian hesitated then straightened, catching sight of me. "You will follow royal orders. That is all."

Fedir looked over his shoulder, catching my eye. "Yes, Your Majesty. Royal orders, as is my duty."

He pulled Killian into a hug, slapping his back with several loud thumps before leaving without another word.

"Is...everything alright?" I asked.

Killian nodded, slipping out of his jacket. "This castle is full of those who are loyal to the crown. Many have grown quite fond of their new queen."

I reached his side, taking his hand. "No matter what happens with your power tomorrow, know that I won't leave you. I love this kingdom and I'll help you rule our people as best we can."

He lifted me into his arms. "I know. You're the queen they deserve."

He kissed me as he took us to bed, laying me down softly and helping me out of my dress, his mouth trailing over every part of me he exposed.

He slipped inside me where I loved him most. "Killian," I breathed, "I'm so, so sorry—"

His mouth consumed mine, cutting me off entirely. His tongue delved deep and I had no way to tell him the words that repeated in my head.

I'm sorry I failed.

I'm sorry I'm not enough to save you.

I'm sorry I didn't get here sooner.

Just a little longer, and I would have had it. Just a little more time and I'd find his name, saving him from a cruel Goddess and my sister from an earlier death than what she deserved.

I should have insisted on completing our marriage the moment I came of age—the moment I met Seraphine and understood the happiness she would bring my brother.

I should have—

Killian thrust hard, filling me completely and I cried out, gripping the corded muscles of his arms.

"Stay with me," he whispered, meeting my gaze in another deep thrust. "My Morella, My Goldling..." His strong hands swept over my face. He didn't mention the tear he caught, only set his forehead to mine as he thrust deep again. "Stay with me, here, in this moment together."

I nodded, breathing him in, loving all of him as he fucked me so tenderly.

The pleasure he brought built slowly and we savored it together as he held me and I held him.

He didn't ask me what his name was.

He didn't tell me I knew it.

A spark of fear hit me as I wondered why, but it was quickly overcome with all-consuming pleasure as his pace picked up and I didn't know where he ended and I began.

We came together, and he kissed me hard, my own kiss in return just as fierce. He pulled me up and offered me a cup of cool fresh water which I gulped down entirely.

My husband whispered sweet things in my ear as he pulled me to his chest and my body felt heavy, drooping. Suddenly, I was too exhausted to keep my eyes open.

The last thing I heard before I drifted to sleep in his arms was his last confession to me. "It was worth it. The pain, the loneliness, the fear. I'd go through it all again to make you my wife. My Morella...My Goldling."

"*MY QUEEN.*"

I frowned at the voice, my eyelids heavy, my body stiff and unmoving.

"*Morella,*" the voice continued, this time shaking my shoulders. "Wake up, Your Majesty. Please!"

The break in the voice at the final word swept into my thoughts, contorting that line of a dream to the harsh cut of reality. My eyes flew open and I blinked in a blurry fog.

"Fedir?" I croaked.

"I'm sorry, but you must get up. He's already gone."

I jolted upwards, my limbs oddly heavy. "Killian?" I searched the bed, finding only rumpled sheets and my own nakedness. Fedir turned, holding my crimson nightgown out for me to slip into.

"What time is it?" I puffed, adjusting the silk to fit my wings.

"Dawn approaches, but I couldn't do it. I couldn't follow his orders and I knew you'd hate me forever if I did."

I paused, sweeping my hair into a loose braid, pulling on his shoulder to face me. "What orders?"

"He didn't want you to see...what would happen when you failed this morning."

Sheer, undiluted panic flooded my veins. I raced to my journal, finding a note and a small bottle of shimmering blue liquid.

Moh Dhóches,

I could not leave this world without ensuring what you needed from me was at least partially given. This potion will prolong your Seraphine's life by a few decades at least. Have her drink it all and she will remain the same age for an undetermined amount of time. Do not ask where it is from or what it cost to retrieve it. Our kingdom's coffers are plenty.

Enjoy your life. Enjoy your Queendom. I have no doubts you will rule as a fair and prosperous Queen. If I may catch a glimpse of your life as I go beyond the Veil, then I hope I have proven myself a worthy man of it.

Do not dwell on the impossible bargain I offered you. It was impossible for a reason.

Céad ensured this task could not be completed, and it is why I must leave you now. Know that Captain Fedir was only following orders. He is a loyal man and will serve you well in the years to come.

I love you, My Morella. I love you, My Goldling.

Time was not on our side, but my heart always will be.

Gib an coich sig thist,

Killian

Until we meet again.

The note dropped from my shaking hands and I turned on my heels. "What did you do?" I whispered, rage fueling the movement in my body.

Fedir stood near the door, paler than I'd ever seen him, with dark circles under his reddened eyes as if he'd been crying. "I concocted a powder that would force you to sleep through all of it."

My voice came eerily steady. "All of what?"

He gulped. "Killian knows Céad will kill him the moment this morning's sun hits his face. He tried to save you from seeing what he himself has seen three times before—the dead body of the one you love."

I shook my head slowly. "She's just taking his power. He never said anything about—"

"He didn't want you to know. He thought he was saving you from needless pain, but I couldn't do it. He's my friend and I love him, too."

He rushed forward, grabbing my bare shoulders and shaking me. "Save him, Morella. *Please.* You were meant to save him."

Just like that, I was gone, racing through the dark hall, down the stairs—so many *fucking* stairs. I would have given up my wings in an instant if it meant I could shift like the Forestfae and reach the cliffside faster.

My feet bare, my heart pounding, I raced to save the man who was mine. I claimed him, I loved him, I worked to break down every one of his fears, and I was not spending the rest of my life without him. I was not ruling this kingdom *without him*.

His name, his name, his name.

I knew it. He said I knew it.

My lungs were on fire as I rounded another corner, fast approaching the door to the library.

His name, his name, his *name*.

He'd given me everything I needed and I thought that meant the language of Céaduah. I thought he meant I knew his name intimately because I was so quick to learn the language of Céad.

Morelli. Morella.

I yanked open the library door, half flying down the winding staircase.

Morelli. Morella.

Intimately. I knew it *intimately*.

The jagged stones of citrine crystals hummed in the barest light as dawn continued its approach. I ran through the cavern, ignoring the cuts opening again on my feet.

I knew it. *I had to know it.*

I reached the end of the tunnel and shifted into a raven, my golden wings alight just as the first break of orange rays hit the citrine in the cliffside, signaling Killian's last chance at someone saving him from the death that called his name in secret.

Fighting the concoction that had sent me so deep into sleep, I urged on, soaring over the valley below, spotting the cliffside where my husband kneeled, waiting for his fate.

His fate.

Moh Dhóches.

It was the only name he'd given me that was in Céaduah. He couldn't say his own name, so that wasn't it. But the others...

He called me Morella. He called me Goldling.

The first, I'd known all my life. Intimately. The second I'd known since the moment our bargain was struck and I became the only hope he had left.

My Morella, My Goldling.

Morelli and ór.

Morelliór.

Golden Mushroom.

That day I'd shouted Morelli across the cliffs, he'd been so proud. He'd praised me over and over, telling me how smart I was because I'd been so close.

So fucking close.

I beat my wings faster, though they felt like they were lighting on fire, and ignored the protest of my lungs, nearing the cliff's edge as he came more into view. The sun's rays crept forward as he sat on the edge of the cliff, just waiting to meet his fate as if he'd already accepted death.

Well, I hadn't and it was I who controlled his fate.

I shifted mid-air, the golden sun hitting my back as I shoved him. Hard.

We tangled together, rolling away from the cliff's edge, but I was faster, pushing him back down as he began to rise.

I spread my wings tipped in gold, rushing to the very edge of the cliff and shielding the man I loved from a fate I would not allow.

"MORELLIÓR!" I screamed. The sound of his name echoed across the Citrine Cliffs, repeating over and over and shifting the wind that blew my hair across my face.

I repeated again and again the name I understood now was his.

"Morelliór! Morelliór! Morelliór!"

With all the breath I had left in my lungs, I screamed in perfect Céaduah, "His name is Morelliór and he is mine! You will not take him from me!"

"*Morella.*" He pulled me to him, turning me with a stream of tears down his cheeks. Cupping my face, he kissed me, whispering over and over, "You did it. You did it, you did it, you fucking did it."

I pushed him back and slapped him across the cheek. "I almost didn't, you absolute ass! How could you—"

A figure loomed at the tree line, walking slowly with golden curls I knew.

"Alista?" I breathed, stepping in front of Killian.

As she took a few more steps toward us, other figures came into view. The three guards I'd met when I arrived at the castle. One of the maids and a stable boy—several more I recognized but could not name.

Each Changelingfae neared, disappearing entirely when they touched Alista until all were gone but her. And then she changed, transforming into the most beautiful woman I'd ever seen.

Her hair remained in golden ringlets that flowed down her back like a shimmering, woven river. Her skin darkened further to a deep brown like night itself could never compare. An aura of gold graced over her shimmering gown and eyes, blinding as the sun.

"Céad," I whispered, attempting to shove Killian again as he grabbed my waist, pulling me behind him.

"Our bargain is over, Goddess of the Changelingfae," he began. "She has discovered my true name and my power has returned. You cannot harm me."

I skirted out of his grasp, blocking him with my body and wings as Céad continued forward as if all the time in the world was meant for her. "You cannot take him from me!" I shouted.

A grin, broken through madness, swept over her face as she withdrew a dagger from her hip and plunged it straight through my chest.

CHAPTER 34

Killian

SOMEWHERE, A MAN SCREAMED. SOMEWHERE, A MAN fell, catching his love in his arms as blood trickled from her body. So much blood.

That man could not be me.

I'd done this before, I could not do it again.

Not with her.

Anyone but her.

The Changlingfae Goddess known as Céad, knelt, sweeping the hair from Morella's face as she tilted her head—that same maddening smile I'd seen before gracing her face.

"Save her," I seethed in Céaduah, gripping tightly to my lover's skin as her breath sputtered and blood dripped from her lips.

"I needed an heir, Morelliór," she cooed in her language—in that same singsong voice that had haunted me for years.

I watched in fear as Céad's aura pulsed, fading in and out as Morella's eyes dimmed. "SAVE HER!" I bellowed, reaching for the Goddess and meeting only a wisp of air.

Her form faded more, bits of her skin floating away in the shifting breeze.

She couldn't go.

She couldn't just leave.

She'd harmed the child of another Goddess and that fate was the final death.

But she couldn't just take Morella from me now. I gritted my teeth in panic, pulling Morella to my chest, sobs wracking my body.

"You need not beg me to save your lover this time, Morelliór," she called, half of her body leaving in golden flecks of dust. "She accepts the power to save herself. You have found one worthy."

I shook my head, my chest heaving with rocking cries, unable to save my love, even with my power fully returned.

The last of Céad drifted, leaving the cliffside as if she'd only ever been a spirit upon the wind.

No, no, no, no, no.

I laid Morella gently onto the rocky earth, someone's hands —my hands—pulling the knife from her chest and pressing on the spill of blood from her wound, pouring every last ounce of power I may yet yield into her skin.

But I was not gifted with the magic that could heal.

And Morella's eyes were already closed.

And I could not save her.

I brought her to my chest again, falling back and pressing her face against my skin, heaving in the sorrowful sound of a man who would not survive such a blow.

The tears that left my eyes blurred my vision as I stared at her brilliant golden wings—each feather a soft glimmer in the morning light of dawn.

Each golden feather.

Solid gold.

I gasped at the sight, that bastard I called hope slicing through my chest as Céad's words echoed in my head.

You have found one worthy.

The stream of power that radiated around Morella's body

gathered above her open wound, closing her clean-cut skin, reversing the damage done by the Goddess of the Changelingfae.

Her body rose from my arms, floating above the blood stained ground as her wings of pure gold hummed, beating stronger, faster. That thin line of shimmering power grew around her, encasing her body like a shell. She spun in midair and all I could do was stare, mesmerized, allowing myself to feel that hope she'd given me months ago in a western tower as she'd shown me her true heritage as Changelingfae. I'd known then that she was the best chance I'd ever had to find the one person who could discover what was hidden from the world.

You have found one worthy.

Céad had been right there all along. Watching the castle. Watching me.

"Morella," I whispered, on my knees, ready to beg for her to stop, to return wholly to me. "Morella, please."

Her spinning halted suddenly and she fell to the ground in a heap of gold feathers and crimson silk. I rushed to her, but before I could touch her skin, her wings flared in a blinding light as the sun reflected off each golden barb.

She slowly sat upright, turning to me with eyes shining brilliant as the sun.

I cast my gaze downward, shielding my eyes. "Morella?" I called, reaching out for her to take my hand.

Warm fingers I knew threaded through mine, and a fierce cry left my chest as I pulled and pulled, bringing her to me, cradling her head in my hands. Her glowing aura of gold dimmed and I pulled her face back to see that she was alive and well.

Better than well.

Her glowing eyes returned to the ones I'd memorized and she blinked up at me. "I think I died," she whispered, all traces of the blood on her lips gone.

"How do you feel?"

She sat back, staring down at her chest and sweeping a hand over her mended skin. "Powerful."

I laughed, pulling on her hips to straddle my waist. "Do you know what happened to you, Moh Dhóches?"

She nodded, looking over my shoulder to the glistening cliffs. "Alista—I mean...Céad needed an heir. I'd proven myself worthy and so...she hurt me. She hurt me to destroy herself. But her power..."

I gulped, nodding and finishing for her. "Her power transferred to her chosen heir." I grinned. "You, Morella." I swept a hand through her hair. "*You* are now the Goddess of the Changelingfae."

Her hands drifted over my skin. "Morella, Goddess of the Changlingfae, daughter of the Ravenfae Goddess, sister of the Cursebringer, wife of...of..." she laughed lightly, the sound lifting my heart, making me feel as if I could soar above the clouds as she could. "What do I call you now that I know all of your names?"

I shook my head, huffing a laugh. "I don't fucking care." I pulled her closer, refusing to relinquish my grip. "As long as one of them is 'husband'."

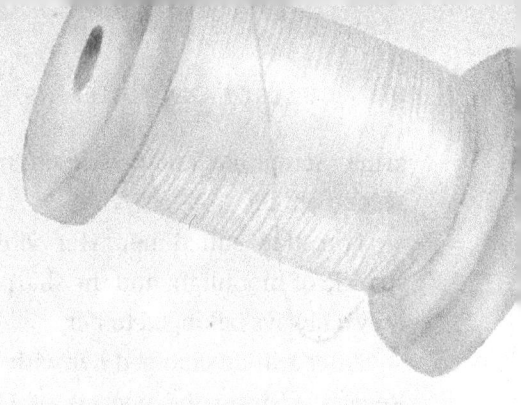

Epilogue

SEVEN MONTHS LATER

MY HUSBAND DANCED WITH ME AT OUR WEDDING.

Our *second* wedding, for he insisted the first could not count.

The first was not full of him declaring his love for me.

The first was not him meeting me halfway down the aisle because, as he whispered in my ear, "You look good in red and nothing."

And the first was not me laughing and pulling on his shoulder so he could bend down for me to whisper, "Are those really the only two?"

And the first was not him breathing back, "Not sure. Let me see the second one again."

Our first wedding was not an open circle of our people giving us room to dance together in a candlelit ballroom as he swept me across the floor, knowing perfectly well the steps to the dance of the Changlingfae—my people now that I was given the power and title of their Goddess.

And the first was not his hand on my belly—our first child just beginning to make himself known to all who noticed such things.

My sister did, of course. The moment she swept me into her

arms, Seraphine knew—herself much further along with her second child.

Forestfae suited her. Her violet eyes now shown with a sparkle of moonlight and the sharp point of her ears seemed as if they'd always belonged to her.

After Killian changed her with his unique power, we traveled Revelry, visiting the pockets of Changelingfae that had made their communities outside of the Citrine Cliffs. I'd been met with awe and acceptance to my people as well as all the other Goddesses of the Realm...except one.

"Do you think she's safe, wherever she is?" I asked my brother, resting after so much dancing, and watching my sister-in-law and my husband bow gracefully to each other before the next dance began.

"Our mother is old, lest you forget, Morella," Korven answered, chuckling as Fedir held Avici in his arms and danced her around the ballroom floor, laughing as her raven black wings flapped in his face.

Korven paused for a moment, taking in my golden wings again. "You can't feel her? Even as a Goddess of the Veil?"

I shook my head. "None of the other Goddesses know, either. No one has heard from her in so long..."

He put his arm around my shoulder, lying his cheek atop my head. "She'll come back to us. She always comes back."

I nodded and sighed. "At least I'll always have you here. And the family you've given me."

He kissed my temple. "It wouldn't be what it is without you. I would not have my Seraphine for as long as I live without what you did."

"I knew it would all work out, big brother." I grinned up at him, seeing the same eyes of our mother. "I just knew it would."

meaning. Available on Kindle Unlimited and major book-sellers.

If you enjoyed this book, (or any book!) I'd like to encourage you to rate/review it. Algorithms from sites like Amazon, Goodreads, and Barnes & Noble base their recommendations of books from a book's number of reviews and ratings. These reviews and ratings are especially important to indie authors like me who do not have high budgets or marketing resources to gain a large readership. We depend on people like you to help us, so thank you for your support. Happy reading!

Acknowledgments

Acknowledging all the wonderful people who have made this book complete is basically impossible, but I'm going to do my best.

First off, I want to thank my readers. You are each a shining light for me, loving my writing, adoring my characters, and impatiently waiting for my next books. I don't know what I've done to have captured so many lovely people's attention, but I'm here for it. I write these stories for you and for me and for anyone in the future who finds my work. Thank you for the DMs. Thank you for the shares, and general squealing along with me at these characters and all the emotions they put us through.

Thank you Rachel. I love you, my soul sister.

Thank you Elaina. I needed your encouragement for this one more than anything before.

Thank you Desiree. I loved adding a little of your own story into this one.

Thank you Cindy and Katie. You both constantly talk about my books to people you know and people you don't—I see it and I'm in awe every single time that I get to have such supportive readers like you.

Thank you Reed. Thank you Violet.

And thank you Will. When you saw your mama sobbing, you nudged my shoulder with the most encouraging words I've ever heard you say. How could I love you more, my sweet boy, who has so much to learn but knows this with clear assurance: Your mama works hard and hard work pays off. Thank you for being so proud of me and assuming I will achieve all of my dreams just because you look up to me as your mom. I love you so much.

About the Author

Chelsey Ann Tompkins was born to be a storyteller, specializing in tales of magic and swoon-worthy romance. Her adolescence was spent reading countless historical romance novels and classic literature, leading to a love of brooding men and strong-willed female characters. When she is not dreaming up heartbreaking romance stories, you can find her brewing yet another vanilla latte, at the library with her kids, or reading while indulging in the blissful silence a bubble bath provides. She resides near Seattle with her husband and two children.

instagram.com/chelseyanntompkins
tiktok.com/@chelseyanntompkins
threads.net/@chelseyanntompkins

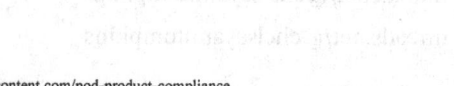